T0203145

PRAISE F

"Confessions of sexbot addicts, confessions of divination addicts, mighty marvels fighting, further rabbit god incarnations, cosmological parables that gust inverted the umbrella of your epistemology— Shen's stories are literary NDEs where worlds dissolve and shift but the rock-steady sadness does not. *Vague Predictions & Prophecies* is a sensitive, risky, and brilliant collection of dazzles engineered to wink out of a profound and dark terrain."

— **EUGENE LIM, AUTHOR OF *DEAR CYBORGS* AND *SEARCH HISTORY***

"Women stand like scarecrows in a pasture outside of town; boys tip them over like cows. Archangel Gabriel slams his head into a wall, over and over again. A single orange geranium peeks out from underneath snow. And right in front of everybody, a mother begins to eat her hand on the train. In Daisuke Shen's *Vague Predictions & Prophecies*, transformations are violent/painful, passion is revenge/playful, and the world can end anytime— but love is forever. An inspiring debut—so alive and full—Daisuke Shen's a genius."

— **ASHLEIGH BRYANT PHILLIPS, AUTHOR OF *SLEEPOVERS***

"Addictive, elegant and juicy... These stories feel limitless and buzzing. They move coolly between time, culture and literary form, exploring the triviality of it all. Shen's writing is sweet and eerie; their characters strange and ordinary, on the edge of miracle or violence. *Vague Predictions & Prophecies* perfectly captures Shen's talent and versatility as a writer—I'm sitting on the edge of my seat for more."

—JAMIE MARINA LAU, AUTHOR OF
GUNK BABY* AND *PINK MOUNTAIN
ON LOCUST ISLAND

"Daisuke Shen is the best and smartest talent working in the short long form today. Shen's characters satisfy both expected and eccentric, terrestrial and astrological, humanoid and primal demands. Sharp in pungency and volatile like soy nuts in their composition, Shen's recklessly unforgettable characters are wasabi-like in their delivery and psyche-stimulating in their inventions. Shen's stories capture their suffering, distress, oddity, madness, futility, dejection, love, and misery with depths of empathy, sharp honesty, and clear foreshadowing. These stories ooze with nail polish, sandpaper, with horseradish roots. *Vague Predictions & Prophecies* is a rice cake on fire."

— VI KHI NAO, AUTHOR OF *WAR IS*
NOT MY MOTHER

"With a strangeness and risk so refreshing it recalls the best of Kelly Link's short fiction, or the ghosts of Alice Munro and Ryu Murakami commingling in an expanse of broken promises to late capital's rush for incorporation, Daisuke Shen's stories beg us to maintain a visceral attachment to absurdity as the only true contestant against the lackluster psychic domination of the real."

—JOSEPH EARL THOMAS, AUTHOR OF *SINK* AND *GOD BLESS YOU, OTIS SPUNKMEYER*

"Daisuke Shen's stories are strange, funny, beautiful, and terrifying. Characters include tortured lovers, migrants, zombies, video games, teenagers practicing a debauchery of sadness, and different versions of God, all serving as witnesses in a cross-examination of human nature.

Vague Predictions & Prophecies is a constant play of styles, genres, the frontiers between nightmares and reality, and the power of silence. The marvelous thing about these stories is that they use the reader's own blank spaces to convey horror not as an extraordinary occurrence, but as a portrait of everyday life."

— YURI HERRERA, AUTHOR OF *SIGNS PRECEDING THE END OF THE WORLD* AND *TEN PLANETS*

"Daisuke Shen's *Vague Predictions & Prophecies* are stories that carve themselves into your bones, tapping into some primal energy that is both completely relatable yet singularly strange. Their way of writing about the world is so big-hearted, so fucked up, so tender and also so brutal."

—JULIET ESCORIA, AUTHOR OF
YOU ARE THE SNAKE

VAGUE PREDICTIONS & PROPHECIES

For all those who have lived on the outskirts of sanity, &
for those seven years

VAGUE PREDICTIONS & PROPHECIES

DAISUKE SHEN

FICTION

CONTENTS

THE PASTURE

Everyone agreed that the South was a terrible place to live, but an even worse place to die. The worst part is that there was no way out, at least none that we could see. We were doomed.

That's why from the time we were seven until now, we had decided, "fuck it." Life fucks us, so we'll make it just as miserable as we are. We got all the easy stuff out of the way early—dine-and-dashing, knocking over mailboxes, challenging kids at school to fight Griff for the low price of $5. If they didn't want to fight, we would hold them down and dig their wallets out from their pockets and grab whatever we could find: $10, Zaxby's coupons, GameStop gift cards from moms and aunts and grandads. We had even gotten a couple of GameBoys out of it. Most kids chose to give us the $5, and Griff would wail on them until they were gasping and puking up blood on the sidewalk outside.

None of the teachers wanted anything to do with it. They were pussies and scared and so was every other adult in this town. They went to the grocery store and bridal showers; church and Bible study, where they would pray that God would handle it. Handle us. And one day he did.

Last Monday, a woman that Christian's family knew had shown up on their doorstep, telling them that she was considering reporting all of us to the local authorities. Her son Joseph had been one of Griff's victims two weeks ago at school, she said, had come home sobbing with a dislocated shoulder. Apparently, he had kept his mouth shut for a couple of days before naming us: Christian Forrester. Danny Wyatt. Del Thomson. Griff Abel. Rhett Collins. Fucking snitch had told her everything about us, the fights, the bets, all of it. Mr. Forrester almost killed Christian that night after he found out, held a gun to his head and asked if this was how he raised his boy, to be an ugly little bitch that wasn't good for nothing except making himself feel better about his sorry self by whooping other kids.

So we laid low after that, hoping the lady wouldn't tell. Christian was forced to apologize to Joseph and then was sent off to boarding school somewhere in Rhode Island. The rest of us were shit out of luck, because she ended up telling on us anyway. Lucky for us, Danny's dad was the sheriff. Or so we thought.

"For a while, I told myself that y'all were just doing kid stuff, it was fine. Needed to get it out the system," Sheriff Wyatt had said to the four of us as we sat in the living room at Danny's house, trying to hide our smirks. "But y'all went too far, and it don't do me or anyone else no good to keep pretending. Your momma," Sheriff Wyatt said, pointing at Griff, "don't need another one of her sons in jail. How do you think it made her feel to find out about this?"

"She done told me how it made me feel," Griff said, his face unmoving. He never showed any emotions at all, never laughed or cried or nothing. The only time I ever saw something human in him was when he was fighting, a strange glint flickering in his eyes that I didn't want to understand.

"And what'd she say?" Sheriff Wyatt asked, leaning forward on the couch.

"She told me she didn't care if I lived or died."

A silence blanketed the room. Sheriff Wyatt coughed.

"Well, now. I think she must have just been...emotional or somethin'. Life ain't been easy for her ever since your daddy passed. But that's besides the point. Starting on Saturday, y'all will be working y'alls little asses at the soup kitchen. Community service might do some good for you."

"Aw, Dad, don't get your panties all up in a wad," Danny complained. "It was only five bucks."

"You live a very privileged little life, boy. And if you don't do as I say, I'll make sure you end up somewhere, just like Christian. 'Cept where I send you won't be anywhere near as good." Danny lost his smile real quick.

After that, we stopped with the fights and tried to make nice with all the teachers and losers at our school. They weren't buying it. Del's mom told him she was proud, that working at a soup kitchen would put the kindness back into our souls. Truth was, I don't think any of us ever had any to begin with. Me, I didn't have anyone telling me nothing. My mom was so looney and out of her mind that she couldn't even register my face sometimes when I walked through the door, so when I confessed all of our sins to her, all she did was smile.

"My baby," she crooned, patting my head. She wasn't even looking at me when she said it; her eyes were focused elsewhere. She pointed at the wall beside the kitchen door, slanted with afternoon light. "You see that angel, son? I see 'em. I know you can't, which is why I'm telling you. And me and you, we're angels too. And God will take us home, and then we'll come back to be in other people's kitchens."

I had no idea what the hell she was talking about, so I just nodded. After a while of patting my head some more, she went over to the wall and started talking to the angel, saying all sorts of crazy stuff about the splendor of the universe and how honored she was that we had been chosen. I slunk back out the door and dipped my head low into the dark.

The next day, we went to the soup kitchen. We spooned out instant mashed potatoes and chili onto people's plates as they walked in, emaciated or pock-faced or just plain sad. It was slow work, and I kept looking at the yellow clock on the wall tick-tick-ticking to see when our shifts would be over.

"Y'all heard about the pastures?" Del said as he dumped chili on a man's plate, splattering some of it onto his shirt. The man was so old and looked up at us with hollow eyes, not even blinking as he moved his tray along. A lot of people looked like that here, a corpse going through the motions. Some of them even looked like my mom, acted like her, babbling and motioning to stuff no one else could see. I hated those women the most.

"What pastures?" Danny asked. He was so quiet when he talked it was funny sometimes how scary he could be. The type of guy who would break someone's fingers, slowly, and he would do it for fun.

"The ones with all the girls in 'em. Standin' there. Just like scarecrows."

"You even know what a girl looks like, Del?" I asked.

Del slammed the top of counter so hard that some of the meatloaf juice jumped and spilled over into the green beans. I waited to see if one of the adult volunteers would come out from the back and give us a scolding, but nobody came.

"Shut the hell up, Rhett. You better watch your damn mouth before I shove this meatloaf down your throat."

"I ain't gonna shut up and you ain't gonna do nothing about it."

Del's head whipped around and I was sure he was going to hit me until Griff spoke up.

"My uncle said he used to go there as a kid. Those pastures behind Reverend Michael's house. Him and his friends would tip 'em over, watch 'em lay there squirming, not able to get up. Said he felt real guilty about it."

"I'll go," Danny said as he nodded at a woman wearing a nightgown, inching her way down the line on crutches. "Rhett, you in?"

I turned to look at Griff. Griff was the one who made the decisions for us, everyone knew that. Danny and Del seemed to remember this too, and fell silent.

"Griff," I said as he placed a roll onto a plate, and then another, not looking at us. "What do you think we should do?"

He wiped the sweat from his nose and looked at us with his granite black eyes, a thin smile spreading across his face. The one he had when he was fighting. I realized in that moment why his momma was so convinced he was a monster. She'd beaten him every night as a kid, trying to get the demons out. The welts on his body were everywhere.

The one on his right arm gleamed in the light, pink and puffy, as he continued to place the rolls on the plates. He still wasn't looking at us, and I wondered if Del had made a mistake.

"We'll go tonight," Griff said. And that was that.

I don't know what I was expecting when the four of us arrived at that field. Danny was on a strict probation, but his dad fell asleep early most nights anyway, a bottle of whiskey in the crook of his arm. All of us were wearing caps and black clothing, as Griff had instructed, so that we wouldn't be recognized so clearly if anyone came by.

As we stood there, listening to the sounds of each other's breathing and the slow, syrupy sounds of the water from the creek nearby, I realized that I didn't really want to be here at all. Maybe, I thought as Griff dug out the flashlight from his backpack, cursing as it blinked in and out, maybe that it would just be a joke. That Griff's uncle was just a jokester and that I could go back home, take a shower, wake up tomorrow and forget that we had ever come here. But it was important to act tough, and so when the flashlight finally turned on, the white light cutting through the dark, I didn't turn away.

There were all different types of women. Short, pretty, tall, fat, skinny, old, young. Wearing business uniforms or wedding dresses or jeans. Some of them had on nothing but underwear. I felt my face grow hot. Beads of sweat dripped down my face but I didn't dare move. I had to wait for Griff's call.

"Are they real?" Del asked.

"'Course they're real," Danny said, and though his voice always sounded like a whisper, I thought I heard it shaking. "Their eyes are moving."

When I looked back up I saw that Danny was telling the truth. They were blinking, wincing away from the harsh glare. Some of them seemed to be waking up, their eyes fluttering, still half-closed. Except for the woman on my right. She was wearing pink, lacy lingerie. Her blue eyes met mine and didn't look away, and inside of them, I saw a terrifying, haunting grief.

The rest of us watched as Griff hopped the fence, holding our breath as he tipped over a woman who looked like a flight attendant. She fell onto the grass, her limbs unmoving at first. I thought that maybe she had died; but then again, how was I supposed to know if they were alive in the first place?

"Fuckin' spooky, man," Del whispered. Danny elbowed him and told him to stop being a pussy.

"Shut up, faggots," Griff said.

As soon as he said it, I saw a shudder go through the woman's body before disappearing again. I saw Danny's breaths, white and wispy in the cold night air, grow faster with anticipation. Suddenly, her neck shot up with a *crack*. She stared at us, her gaze hollow, as she began writhing on the ground like a centipede, her limbs grasping at anything, anything on the ground around her that might be able to save her.

Her movement broke the spell of silence. I could smell everyone's sweat and excitement as Del whooped and jumped over the fence, Danny following after him. *They've fucking lost it,* I said to myself as I watched them, fighting to see who could push all of those ladies over the fastest, laughing as the women rolled around on the ground, unable to speak, their mouths open like dumb animals gasping for air.

"Come here, Rhett," Griff said. He was pointing to the

woman wearing the lacy bra and panties, who was still staring at me, now her eyes were huge and full of fear. "Seems like this one wants you."

I should've said no. I should've just left right then and there, but I knew that if I did that, Griff would want to hurt me the next day. I had to obey. I placed my leg over the fence, then the other.

"That's it," Griff said, and then I felt his hands on my back as he thrusted me toward her. I fell right into her body, my face landing between her breasts.

Griff laughed. I couldn't breathe. She smelled like powder and gardenias, her skin cold against my cheek. I fell backwards as Griff laughed again, his flashlight sweeping across the pasture. Now I could see all of them at once, though I really wish I hadn't. They were tugging at the women's clothes, trying to see what would come off. Del removed a woman's stockings with his teeth. From my right, I swear I could hear the sound of a belt buckle snapping.

"Stop," I said as Danny ripped open one of their blouses, his hands burrowing into her body. "Stop, stop, I don't like this." My voice didn't sound like my own, and it rang hollow in my skull.

"You want to do it too," Griff said, and I saw that he was on the ground, his hands tugging at the flight attendant's skirt. He took off his t-shirt. In the false light, his collarbones looked so smooth and delicate; the fine, soft black hair of his stomach. A flash of remembrance sparked across my mind: the rare sight of Griff's smile, the slight gap between his teeth when we'd happened upon a turtle in a pond. He'd held it so gently. I'd never thought he was capable of such kind touch.

"Don't you?" He called, and the memory was spurred

back into time, and I was again in the horrific now. "You ever seen a pussy before?"

"No," I said, "no," and then I stopped as I heard shrieking.

Griff paused and turned his flashlight toward the right. Danny, clutching a piece of fabric in his hand, screamed as the woman on the ground unhinged her jaw further as she devoured the rest of Danny's body another howl came from the middle of the field. Del was trying to claw away from the woman whose stockings he had removed, her long acrylic nails digging into his shin. Danny cried again as she continued her slow puncturing up and down his body, a shrill note that dipped into guttural moans before picking up again. Pockets of blood erupted everywhere.

My mind couldn't make sense of anything. I stepped backward, once, twice, as Griff yelled at me.

I realized this was the first time I had ever heard him scared. "Don't you—"

The flight attendant wasn't motionless any more. She was on all fours, hissing, and the flashlight dropped onto the ground right as she pounced on his chest. There was a loud crack, sick and hollow—the sound of splintering bones.

I couldn't see anything but I could hear where the pasture was now moving, alive with women. I started to run before a hand stopped me, landing across my chest.

The beautiful naked woman was looking at me, smiling. Her eyes were so sad, all the empty rooms in the world gathered inside of her irises. I remembered at that moment what my mother had always said about angels, being divinely chosen, and I wanted more than anything for that to be true.

"Please, ma'am," I said. "Please—"

She looked at me with something like sympathy, her mouth pursed and glossed with pink. And then she opened her mouth and screamed.

The scream merged with the sound of a distant truck, its steel body grating against the guard rails before the driver angled it back onto the road. I stood, stunned, unable to move. A terrible pain in my right ear, something singing inside of it. Dizzy, I stumbled over the field of women, unable to take my eyes off of her. I realized that even though I could still see her screaming, I couldn't hear anything anymore, and that both my ear drums had burst.

I jumped over the fence and didn't look back. I ran for what felt like hours through the dark, unsure of where I was going until the sun came up and I collapsed, exhausted and sobbing, onto the road. Eventually, I picked myself up and headed back home, where my mother was sitting on the sofa, waving at me when I opened the door before rushing over to hold me.

"Baby, what's wrong? You can talk to me. I'm right here."

I leaned against her, sobbing. I realized that the smell of the other woman had been familiar to me, although I hadn't recognized it at that time—Ma smelled just like gardenias and baby powder. But I must've forgotten. It was the first time I had allowed her to touch me in eight years.

My hearing came back, but the other boys' never did. People went out to look for them, and I told Danny's dad everything: the pasture, the women, the ripping of the clothing. But when they got to the pasture, everything had been wiped clean. On the news, I saw a reporter speaking to a woman who claimed to have lived at the exact location that the pasture had been for the past decade now. Her eyes, bright and blue, seemed to sparkle a bit when she said she hadn't seen any boys, no, none at all, and as she bent over to pick up something she had dropped, a flash of pink winked back at the camera from beneath her shirt. The interviewer stuttered, embarrassed, and the woman laughed. Despite myself, I started laughing, too, until I was bent over holding my sides, laughing so hard that my stomach hurt, thinking about all the evil in the world and how I had and would always be a part of it. Ma, who had been asleep on her chair, woke up and saw me laughing and started laughing along, too. Our voices ricocheted around the walls, creating a chorus of angels: Ma's dream come true at last.

VAGUE PREDICTIONS & PROPHECIES

Everybody knows that God came first. I should know that better than anyone. And I do *know* that.

But that's not how it feels. It feels like before there was God, there was me. And Lucy.

I don't remember what body I had before this one but I know what my current one is made for, though what that thing is, is hard to describe. I am a rotating hall of mirrors. I am a constantly terraforming cluster of stars. I am a mosaic stitched together from the dreams and imaginations of the entire human population.

In other words, I'm whatever you might think I look like. Whatever version of me exists in your head is right. Strictly speaking, I don't *exist* outside that version of me. I'm a sort of function of you. Of everyone.

For now, you can call me Zedkiel.

I bestow mercy. I govern patience. I grant forgiveness after forgiveness to anyone who may ask for it. I stop a man right before the dagger slits the boy open, the man's hand so warm and shaking inside of mine.

"You've passed the test," I tell him. "God knows you fear him. Let him go."

Afterward, I watch them slaughter the lamb in the boy's place. They begin walking home, but then the man turns back. He is still convinced he has to do it. "God told me," he whispers. He smells like rust. Something dark and frantic squirms within his irises; a sign he is coming undone. "I don't have a choice. I don't have a choice."

"I said you are forgiven. Now go."

He doesn't say anything. He keeps staring at me until the very end as I make my way back into heaven. Even in the skies, I feel as if he is still watching me, though I know that's not possible. I move on.

It is 60 BCE. I am floating above a river, watching the Han dynasty take over the Tarim Basin.

It is 610 BCE. Gabriel visits a man and tells him about God. The man writes it all down. A lot more people get ideas about us, about God.

It is 1700. I am in the background as Fernec Rakozi is hung in Austria.

It is 1859. Emanuel Swedenborg begins to have strange dreams. He documents them, titles the book *Drömboken, or Journal of Dreams*.

It is 1940. Four kids show up with their dogs and find some paintings of us that I saw being made so many years ago.

Things continue on like this, until I meet someone.

Its name is Lucy.

After coming back from Earth one day, I accidentally transfer myself into the corner of the smallest universe I've ever seen. At first, I can't believe it. Angels don't have accidents. We're precise: the only thing I have to do is locate the point on the axis of the heavens where I want to go and there I am. I've been to every single universe. Not just the one humans know. Every single time God created a new one, I visited it. But I check the coordinates on the map again and again. I search through my Scroll, flicking through the list of all 200 billion of them in half a fraction of a second after I've input my coordinates and it comes up with nothing. Cygnus A. Virgo A. Sadonus X. Andromeda A. Canus Major. Forneus. Rade X. Sidal Throne. Akamatsu 3. The Crow cluster.

I try pinging the other angels, pinging God.

But no one responds. Could God have closed himself off from this place? There is no sense of Him anywhere. There are no stars, no planets. It's a deprivation chamber rid even of the omniscient.

Suddenly, I feel myself shaking, different pieces of me flaking off. I'm suffocating. Different body parts fracturing, scuttling, trying to escape.

In the distance, I see something. It has thorns. Tentacles. A mouth full of teeth. I drift toward it as I continue disintegrating. If I disappear, it will be alright. There will always be another angel to take my place. Perform my functions.

The creature in front of me shudders and cloaks itself, vines wrapping around its mouth. It seems angry. I gasp as another wave of pain plunges through me, but perhaps it is just another thing that needs forgiveness, too. Forgiving it will be my final act.

But then I stop. There's something inside of the mouth. It's waving. The vines and tentacles drop down and wrap around the being, attempting to hide it from view. To keep it from coming out.

Suddenly I get a ping. But it's not from God or anyone else I tried to reach, it's not from anyone outside of this universe. It's coming from inside the cage. Meaning, that thing is an angel.

The angel's consciousness is attempting to communicate with mine and I let it in. It seeps inside of me, heavy and claustrophobic. We are entangled now, but at least I'm not dying any more.

"What are you doing?" I ask, but it doesn't respond. Inside of our consciousnesses, an infinite temple forms. Rows of pillars spread before me. Thoughts arrange and re-arrange themselves around me, colors that can't be understood. I try searching for meaning, but it's indescribable.

"Trying to find something?" one thought asks. It darts beneath a shadow before I can grasp it.

I have to go. Report this finding to God. "Let me go," I say, and the thoughts swivel around the pillars, squeezing them so hard they shake. "God will destroy you."

The angel makes a strange sound, a sound like hummingbirds or crisp glittering ice. I snap outside of the temple back into the universe and find that its body is circling around mine, coiling like a snake.

"Maybe he's already destroyed me?"

It sends a new wave of messages, ones that I can comprehend: the angel isn't in here by choice. This thing that they're trapped inside is a prison. The temple turns to stone.

Then all the signals I can't understand come back, whispering like shadows along the floors.

"I bet you don't know what I just did." the angel says as I scurry away again from the dark.

"What are you talking about?"

"The sound I made. Did you understand it? Let me show you."

Something tilts within me. Slowly at first, then faster and faster until the pressure is too much to handle. "Stop," I say. A sudden wave of black washes over me, absorbing me, cracking me open so that I am raw. I scream, my voice rippling through the hollow chamber.

"That was what you call 'fear'," it says. My breath ricochets within my body, unable to escape. "But hey, relax." Another twist and warmth spreads over the black, trapping the fear underneath its sprawl. A twinkling noise emerges somewhere amidst the softness that startles me before I realize it's coming from me.

"What is this?" I say. Bells continue spilling out of me, birds in infinite flight.

"Laughter," it says. "You're experiencing happiness."

Something tugs me downward and suddenly I am staring at the angel's form.

Perfect angles carved out of magnificent crystal that melt into hair and arms and legs. Eyes that weep indigo and peach and charcoal. Clusters of stars collect in chains that wrap around its curves, dispersing before connecting again as it moves toward me.

I can't stop staring. Staring, and laughing, and scared. I want to join our consciousnesses, join my body with its, forever. I feel the urge to kill for it. I would do anything it wanted me to.

Before I can do anything, though, it says, "Here's all the rest."

Fractures web across my body before splintering completely. I watch, an impassive observer, as my form scatters and morphs into different segments and shapes and senses. They shift through and around me, floating around in the galaxy. With what is left of me, my consciousness, I draw close to these fragments to analyze.

Different smells and tastes and sights and sounds are embedded inside each one. Everything has changed. The angel lifts their arms, iridescent threads dangling from its fingers. Gently, it gathers the shards together and begins to weave these re-created parts back into my form.

When the angel is finally done, I know everything about why it is here, what it has done.

"Lucy," I say, grasping at the space between us. "Lucy."

"Come here," Lucy says, and opens its thousand arms wide, reaching through the snapping claws surrounding it. "Feel all of it."

Though I cannot make contact with them through the barriers, it's enough. I feel everything Lucy. I cry and laugh and scream and moan and hiss. Lucy murmurs, telling me how glad they are to see an angel for the first time in a millennium, but I'm not thinking about anything else. We're so close that it's as if our faces are almost touching. Its mouth curves, the shape of a swallow in flight.

"I'm lucky that it was you," Lucy says. The swallow dives inside my throat, trilling.

For the first time in my life, I feel this.

I feel like Zedkiel.

I stay there for days. Months. Years. I don't know.

Lucy talks so fast, telling me secret after secret as if scared that if they don't tell me now, they'll forget. But I'll remember. If I had been smart, I'd have erased them from my memory. But it would've still been pointless.

They pause at one point to apologize for how much it's talking, but I don't have anything to say. All I want to do is listen, to them, forever. The only thing that worries me is that the being enclosing them is no longer reacting. Its jaws lay slacked, no longer snapping at me.

"I saw a human one day, and I felt sorry for it. It looked so...lonely." Lucy looks down. I want so badly to touch them, to stroke them, so I mime the motions. Their voices echo into the emptiness. Lucy continues talking, not looking up. This is the first time I've ever seen them ashamed.

"What's wrong?"

"I gave them something."

"What?"

"I don't want to say."

"You can tell me anything. I promise. I'll never think poorly of you. Ever."

"You don't know that. You only learned how to feel disgust just a moment ago."

"It doesn't matter," I say, my voice rising. "I don't care. I love—"

"Don't say things you don't understand," Lucy snaps at me. It hurts. They gather themselves into a ball, their sides growing sharp. "Don't ever say things before you're sure of them."

We are quiet for a moment. The monster's breathing is slow and muted in its sleep.

"Okay. I won't keep asking. And I won't say anything like that again."

Lucy looks at me with their thousands of eyes. Each of them is welling with tears.

"I taught them what I taught you."

Despite myself, despite what I want, I feel myself recoiling. Lucy notices, of course.

"And here you were, about to say you loved me," they say in a mocking voice. The pastels of their eyes mix into one another, and soft waterfalls of color fall around us.

"How could you?" I manage to say. "Humans are... humans were..."

"What do you mean? Were you happy before this, not feeling anything? No, you weren't. You didn't even know what happiness was. It's a human emotion, right? Emotions are what destroy them. That's why they're so evil, according to *him*," they hiss. The waterfalls all turn the color of blood. "But without them, you're just a shell. And if you didn't know shame, didn't know evil, you could do things even more vile than you could possibly imagine. More than you've ever seen in your entire life."

I still don't know what to say.

Lucy keeps talking.

"I'm the reason for all of this," they say, laughing. They heave themselves upward, a tree unrooting itself in a storm. "That's what he says. But why create these vessels, puppets forced to worship you without even knowing why? You want to know what selfishness is? You want to know what evil is? It's the one that you've been serving all these years."

"Shut up," I say. "Shut up, Lucy."

"Maybe you'd like to go back to that, too. Not knowing, not having a sense of who you are. Just a *function*, a thing that serves a *purpose*. A dog so loyal that it wouldn't even care if its owner was the one who skinned and boiled it alive. At least it would be him, right? At least you could die at your master's hand. You'd roll and pant and jump around, and even worse, you'd convince yourself it was what you wanted, it was your choice."

I fly toward Lucy, but the monster wakes up just in time to swing its enormous, groaning limb into my center, flinging me away.

Lucy just looks at me as I dry heave, muttering things to myself that I can't understand. I can't meet their eyes. They know that I know they're right.

It takes me a while to reintegrate. But once I do, I tell them the truth.

"You did the right thing."

As soon as I say this, I hear a familiar sound. A ping. I whip around and for a moment, I think it's him. Then a name etches itself onto the surface of my scroll.

Michael.

The monster shrieks and lunges at Michael, who throws it to the side as if it's nothing. He's always been stronger than me. Better than me. Better at finding what needs to be found.

"Zedkiel. We're going home," he says. And before I know it, I'm flying. Lucy is still inside of that monster as it threads its limbs inside, tearing Lucy apart. Pieces of Lucy drift up all throughout the atmosphere toward us as we continue flying upward. I try again to attack Michael, but it's useless. I can't move anywhere but up, unable to do anything but watch as Lucy is punished, their screams mixing with the monster's as he carries me away.

Before I know it, we're back in heaven. The wind breaks on my face, and the clouds curl around me like white smoke. Above us, two peach suns hover as angels fly around them, shadowless. Lucy is so far away.

Then all the angels' heads turn toward mine. The suns flare and aim their rays toward me, and my wings curl as they burn. Michael throws me toward where God is, at the center of the suns. All the angels' faces are blank. They say nothing. And of course they don't. They don't understand how to feel.

"Kill me," I scream at God. "Kill me, you stupid fuck."

All forms of time stop. I am lifted into God, and it is just God and me, alone, cut off from everything. God surrounds me on all sides, a universe in himself. My lungs fill with God. *His* lungs fill with God. I close my eyes and God is etched onto the backs of my eyelids. My muscles tense, God sinks into my bones.

Finally, God speaks. What does he sound like?

You don't want to know.

But I can tell you what he said.

My and Lucy's love for humans is...admirable. So admirable, in fact, that he'll allow us to revert back to the human forms we were birthed from, the ones we've never known. Of course he intended for this to happen; did I really think that anything went without his noticing? He won't make me forget Lucy. I'll get to remember all the moments we spent together, supposedly alone.

Lucy's true punishment wasn't being imprisoned inside of that monster. No, that was just the beginning. We're going to be playing a fun game, you see—a couple of others are going to be coming with me on this mission. They won't know that it's my fault, so I don't have to worry.

What I should worry about is my assigned task. To hunt Lucy down over years, looking in all of the places they will be forced to hide, scrambling from their own kin. I thought that emotions were great, didn't I? But what a fool I was.

In human form, I'll never be able to escape the pain. It will break me slowly, over the years it will take to find them. But at least there's this: After we kill Lucy, we'll get to come back, become angels again. Everyone else will be turned back to normal, but I'll get to still feel everything, all the time. Remembering. Feeling. Those are my gifts and my punishments. I will feel Lucy's death for all of eternity, and I'll never forget them.

And as we all know, God keeps his promises.

Mike is quiet this week in group. This is good because Mike usually never knows when to shut the fuck up. He's always talking about how back in heaven, he's the one who gets to blow the trumpet, God's favorite, blah blah blah.

"I'm listed in the Bible at least 30 times. Maybe even more," he said once during the part of the course where we were focused on "Mindfulness."

Mindfulness means paying attention to things. Trying to be aware of what's going on in your body. You can calm yourself down by closing your eyes and pretending you're walking down a flight of stairs, or that you are a pebble in a middle of a lake, or stroking your fingernail with your nose. Wait. Stroking your nose with your fingernail.

There was complete silence after that. Ariel coughed into his fist. I could see his shoulders shaking, trying not to laugh.

Mike, of course, was oblivious. He sat up higher in his chair.

"Also, did I tell you that God wants me to—"

"Yes, yes, Mike, you've told us about what happens next," Gabe interrupted him. He looked uncomfortable and small. Nothing like the guy I knew back home. Gabe pulled a handkerchief out of his shirt pocket and blew his nose. "And we're all really proud of you. That's another thing you can put on your positive traits list."

Mike grinned, his smile a flash of white veneers, and wrote this down with his glittery purple gel pen. Mike the human is possibly the worst type of guy possible. He takes notes on anything, including the time Gabe talked us through a fire drill.

When we had arrived to Earth that first day, it had been disastrous. I woke up on a floor to see six other human men lying beside me. The one next to me was snoring. His chest was hairy, his hand shoved down his pants as he slept. I flexed my hands. My neck hurt. I continued looking around the room with my terrible human eyesight at the sleeping bodies surrounding me.

I sat up and felt a sharp urge to urinate combined with something hard between my legs. I peeked underneath my shorts and quickly pulled them back up, embarrassed. At least I was well-endowed.

I knew I was going to piss myself if I didn't hurry, but still, it bothered me that I didn't know who was who yet. I poked the hairy guy on my right.

He snorted and then shot up, gasping, going through the same performance I had. Before he got to the dick, I said, "Hey, it's me. Zedkiel."

His breathing remained the same pace, but he looked a bit relieved. He opened his mouth to say something before doubling over. Thin, watery vomit splattered onto the floor.

"Fuck," he said, "fuck, man."

"Let me go see if I can find some water."

I got up and walked around the house. It must have been an old hospital: there were so many rooms, all of them empty, white, sterile. I slunk around, looking into each one. A vending machine rusted and flickering with blue light. A row of old wired phones dangling from the wall. Eventually, I walked into what looked like the kitchen.

A man was standing at the sink, peeling a clementine. Outside of the broken window, I saw a row of antlers—deer ducking their heads into the long grass. They were grossly mutated, enormous in size. One of them looked up at me, startled by the noise. I saw its muscles ripple underneath its skin. But of course they wouldn't hurt us. Animals hadn't been known to attack anyone in centuries.

The man coughed, and I turned to look at him.

"Hey, Zedkiel," he said, smiling. "It's Michael."

My first instinct was to attack him. I imagined myself throwing him into the wall, strangling him and staring into his face while I did it. I wanted to watch his helpless struggling, feel his limbs flail as he lost consciousness. I wanted him to feel the same way that I had when he had taken me back. I felt my hand curl into a fist.

"You fucking—"

He stuck his hand out to me. I stared at it for a minute, blinking. Was he playing some sort of trick on me? But when I looked up at his face, I saw nothing but friendliness. I remembered then that he probably didn't know.

"I know you're probably feeling a lot right now." He popped the naked clementine in his mouth and chewed it whole. *You have no idea*, I thought. "The anger thing, it's weird, right? But don't worry, we're in this together. God told me about how you had accidentally ended up there, with that...thing. And how it attacked you. So I'm saying, I got your back. We're all here for each other. And I'm glad for that."

So he did remember. I felt the anger in me growing hot. His smile hadn't left his face. The hand floated mid-air, waiting for mine to meet it. I forced myself to shake.

"Thanks, Michael."

"Any time, my friend."

Yelling and loud thumps were coming from the room I had left.

"Ah," Michael said, nodding. "They must have woken up."

Everybody was panicking, one huge ball of panic. The hairy guy ended up being Raphael, who had punched a hole through the wall. Someone else was in the corner, hissing to themselves as they rocked back and forth.

After Michael and I settled everyone down, and we learned who was who. All together, there were seven of us: Me. Michael. Raphael. Ariel, who was still talking to himself, pacing around. Gabriel and Joseph, who showed nothing on their faces. Camael, who sobbed each time he opened his mouth. There was nothing beautiful about any of us.

Three years later, as we sat in this circle of uncomfortable white chairs in the remains of the Episcopalian church close by, going through the DBT handbook I had found, I watched Mike smiling, laughing, acting as if he was enjoying all of this. And I had to pretend that everything was alright between us, even as I imagined myself cutting into his throat with a knife.

Raphael got a grip on the anger thing eventually, by which I mean he developed a drinking problem, and the anger turned into sadness. Some days, I would come home and see him passed out on the couch, fifty beer bottles strewn on the floor beside him. I always made sure to leave some water out for him, a washcloth in case he needed it.

I ended up being the one with anger issues. Sometimes I could see the fear on everyone's' faces when I came around, and that made me feel a whole different set of stuff: angry about the fact that they were scared, angry at myself for being scary, angry that I couldn't just kill Michael due to the limitations that God had put on me. Then I would feel sad. We had all been together for so long, in heaven and now here, and I knew that the word for us was "friends." Maybe even "family." I loved all of them, excluding Michael.

Then the sadness would warp into this guilt that pinned me down and made it so that sometimes, I couldn't leave the bed for days, thinking about how much I wanted to hurt myself, how terrible I was for all of it.

And oh, is it lonely.

I try to manage it the best I can, though. I do the skills. I practice gratefulness. I go to a shop that sells recreations of fast food, the kind they had in earlier times, with Raphael, who always gets a double bacon jalapeño burger. You just don't get that kind of stuff in heaven. It's all ambrosia and milk. Some days, I even manage to laugh. I have fun playing video games with Gabriel and Joseph. But I never forget that we're here for a reason. Most of our days not spent in group or eating burgers are spent planning, coordinating, documenting. Trying to find another angel-turned-human.

It's been three years of collecting data, sending reports back to heaven through the Seraphim (so full of it, those guys; but I would be too if I always appeared in a cloud of flames). Gabe says we're getting close.

After our meeting ended, we split into groups and headed out. Gabe and Raphael and Ariel would be heading to the next town over, though we had been there just two days before. Camael and Michael and I would be heading into the old electric plant. Joseph would stay at the hospital.

My body felt heavy under all the gear and weaponry. The electric plant could be toxic so we needed biohazard suits, gas masks. Michael is leading in the front, and I step around the herds of rats, the clicking beetles. Suddenly, Michael stops. He makes a hand signal, telling us to be quiet.

I've spent a lot of time imagining what Lucy looks like. Of course, there was no way I could know what it would look like in human form, but each time we got a potential lead, and went out to survey it, I could tell—at first glance—that it wasn't Lucy. Tall boy with long dreads, cutting through the grass with a machete to find old car parts to sell. Pregnant girl with dead eyes and pock marks on her face, selling angel figurines at an old frozen yogurt shop. Short kid with freckles at the top of an old water tower, screaming for someone to save her. Each time, I would feel relieved. Maybe this could go on forever. Maybe we would never find it.

Tonight, though, I hear something before I see it. It's ducking through the circuitry hanging from the ceiling, jumping so fast that we can barely see it. Camael throws a flash bomb toward it, and a face appears before being written over by the dark.

Lucy as a human woman looks tired. So tired. Her face is round. Deep purple circles form hollows underneath her eyes. Her hair is long and tangled, her shoulders curving toward the earth. Despite all of this, Lucy is beautiful. So, so beautiful.

Michael pings Joseph and asks him to scan the target, see if it matches with any of the information God has given us, but before he can respond, it's gone. Camael curses as Joseph's voice circulates in all of our heads: *We've found it.*

I realize that I'm feeling things by the way my body reacts: shaking, nauseated, I force myself inside. *I feel fear*, I say to myself. *I am experiencing panic. I am going through the motions of grief. I am angry.*

I am able to locate another feeling. It's inappropriate but it's there.

Most of all, most inappropriately of all, what I feel is happiness. Happiness because finally, after so much time, I've seen her again.

We return to the hospital and they're coming up with a plan. I am numb to the world around me, watching the last shadows of the day crawling on the wall.

"Zedkiel?"

They are looking at me. I don't know how to respond. I can't. I run toward the bathrooms before anyone can stop me and then I'm dry heaving.

Did you think you could avoid this? Forever?

As I stick my fingers down my throat, I feel someone behind me.

It's Michael, leering at me in the dark. Saliva drips down my forearm.

"Zed," Mike says. "I can't believe it. We finally get to go home." He reaches out and begins stroking my back as I stick my head back into the toilet bowl.

"Lucy's been here all along. Just three blocks away from us, this entire time. Who would have thought. Ha ha."

He stops stroking my back and suddenly he's leaning right next to my ear. "That bitch wasn't so hard to find after all, was she?" He laughs.

And suddenly I am on top of Mike with my hands around his neck, then around his skull, slamming his head into the floor as hard as I can. I know that realistically, the wet, slapping noise is his head connecting with the linoleum, just like I knew that the man who I am kneeling over was Mike. But it all feels so far away from me, as if I were watching that boy about to be killed again on that mountain, so long ago.

Someone's arms are around my torso now and I hear the screaming, *stop it, Zed, stop it.* But I don't want to stop. I want to keep squeezing, slamming, bursting until it all comes out. Mike's neck is turning purple. I know God sees everything. I hope he's watching.

Then there is a small thud on the back of my own head and I am out.

In the dream, we're still young, only 500 or so. But Lucy isn't itself: Lucy is the human woman we found yesterday. We're not in that terrible universe, the one where I first met her. Instead, we're on Earth, underneath a shade of trees. Lucy points at a building and asks if I want to see it explode. I tell her, sure. Anything she wants. She lifts her hands then clamps them together fast, like a pair of jaws. The building slowly begins to splinter, suffocating itself, the colors turning from a mottled blue and green into a slick black.

Lucy says that whenever we're together, we escape God's grasp. I don't have a word for the feeling.

She says she loves me.

Are you sure? I ask.

She doesn't answer. She points back to the building, still there, burning. People are inside of it, screaming. I recognize one of the faces as Michael's.

You finish it, she says, stroking my cheek. Go ahead.

And so I do.

I awake to Gabe sitting over me in bed. Lucy's not here. I remember that we're on earth and we've finally found her.

As soon as I try to sit up, Gabe's hand caves into my chest and I'm on my back coughing. Outside of the window, another four-headed deer is digging something out of the ground. When it raises its head, I see a deer fetus hanging from its mouth, similarly deformed. The mother buries it, pushing the earth with her snout, digs it back up, buries it again. Over and over and over, as if hoping that something will change.

"Lot's changed, hasn't it?" Gabe said. He stares at me staring out the window. "Mike almost died, you know. Raf is taking care of the injuries right now. Oughta thank him."

"Don't care. He would've just come back, anyway."

Gabe barked out a laugh.

"Yeah, yeah, everyone knows how much you don't care."

Gabe stands up, starts walking around the room. I peek over my shoulder. His golden brown curls are knotted at the ends, his pure, innocent baby face is twisted in disgust. He spits on the ground. It lands next to the white anthurium.

"Didn't think it would be this bad. Thought maybe three years wouldn't be so bad. But as soon as I'm starting to think it's getting easier, it all gets worse. The nightmares. The terror. I gotta hand it to you and Lucy, though. *Wanting* to feel this stuff, I mean, that's incredible. Truly incredible. How that...monster managed to figure it out, transfer it to you, that's one thing, but the fact you just kept wanting more? Fuck."

I can't do anything but laugh at this point.

"How long have you known?"

"Michael told us two years ago."

It doesn't make sense. Everyone knows that Michael and I have never gotten along. But Raphael. The burgers we ate. Watching shows with Joseph. Gabe and I making up card games with each other, looking out at the red, smoke-filled sky. Why?

Gabe drops down to the floor to sit beside me.

"I don't regret being with her," he says quietly.

I look over at him, but his eyes are closed.

"What are you saying?"

"I'm saying I met someone. Most of us have, at this point. We kept it from each other, obviously. Even if we're technically human now, it's still..." His voice trails off. "It's shameful, you know? But after he told us, Raphael admitted it too. Said he'd been seeing some guy he met while buying food one day in the old shopping center. So then we all started admitting it. What we'd done."

"Why didn't you tell me?"

Gabe laughs. Something's changed in his voice. It's softer now. He feels sorry for me, and I hate it.

"And have it reported back? God lied to all of us. Well, I guess, to everyone except you. We figured that out pretty quick. We figured that once we told you, we'd all meet the same fate that you're bound for. But I guess none of that matters, right? God's been planning this all from the beginning."

Outside, the deer have disappeared. The fetus lies on top of a mound of earth, unburied. Soon, the birds of prey will come. Gabe's hand shoots back out to grab my face and suddenly I am staring right into his eyes.

"Look," he whispers. Inside his pupils, small fireworks erupt. Streams of exploding planets, angels being impaled, people trampled by 30-foot beasts. I see the beginning of time, the middle, the end. I see the stuff written in the Ancient Script, etched into the corners.

And then, I see him crying.

"You wonder why I'm the only one of us who kept these eyes?" he says. The frenetic orchestra of light inside won't stop. "You want to know why he made me keep them down here?"

"Why?"

Gabe laughed, his hand tightening around my jaw. "I have no clue. But I know I have to relive it, every single day. The stuff that happened, the stuff that hasn't even happened yet."

Gabe lets go. I listen to him take deep breaths in and out, inhale through his nose, exhale through his mouth.

"I don't regret being with her," Gabe says again.

"I'm sorry." The words feel pointless coming out of my mouth.

"I'm not like you, though." He spits onto the ground, as if expelling the thought from his body. "What she and I had, it was pure. So was the kid."

I don't need to ask to know that the kid's probably not around.

"He won't let me find out. I can flip through every single human left on this planet, all of their names and faces and locations, but I can't find hers. The kid, for all I know, is in some zoo somewhere."

Gabe turns around. In one quick motion, he slams his head against the wall. *Thud. Thud. Thud. Thud.* I jump up and grab him, but he won't stop. Blood runs down his forehead and drips onto the floor. My body convulses along with his, a reminder that we're more alike than he'd like to believe.

"Gabe, come on, man. It's okay." But he's lost.

"Gabe!" I say, and I force him to look at me like he just did. The centuries trapped inside his eyes are distorted now, like static.

"You're okay. You're safe. You're safe. It's not happening anymore. You're right here with me."

A shudder runs through the floor and I hear people enter. Ariel holds a bowl of water, telling Joe and Raf to wrestle Gabe away from the wall. He looks over, motions with his chin for me to join them.

Together, we dunk his head into the water and hold it there as he jerks around, kicking over pots, empty cabinets.

"Relax," Ariel murmurs. "Relax."

Bubbles erupt from the surface.

"Go get the tranquilizer," I say, but before anyone can move, Cam is in the room flicking a needle and driving it into Gabe's arm. Slowly, his muscles relax and he falls limp. We heave him to the next room and drop him onto the bed. His eyes flutter for a moment, confused, before closing. The fireworks are gone.

"Getting tired of this shit," Joe says, slapping the doorframe hard as he walks out. Cam doesn't say anything as he leaves, but when he glances up at me, I finally see it:

This whole time, I thought they were scared because they didn't understand. But what they're scared of is how much they do.

"Think we're getting pretty good at this whole baptism thing?" Raf asks, and I look up to see his weak smile.

I pick up a waxy-leafed plant that's drifted in from outside, run my fingers over it.

"Tell me what this feels like," I ask, holding it out to Raf.

Raf closes his eyes, taking one of the leaves in his palm.

"It's smooth. The hairs make it soft. Cold." He brings it up to his nose. "It smells like the earth. There's ridges in the middle."

"That's good. That's what I thought, too."

Raf opens his eyes again as he plucks the leaf and puts it in his pocket.

"To add to my collection," he says lightly before his voice changes. "We don't have much more of those syringes left, you know."

"I know."

"I'm sorry."

"Don't be."

Raf opens his mouth, then closes it again. He shakes his head.

"Say it."

Raf clears his throat. "A prophecy came to me last night."

"Bullshit."

"Look, I know he said no abilities, I know, but come on. Look at Gabe's eyes. And we've all seen the growths on Joe's shoulders."

I had. Two small pyramids had emerged recently on Joe's back. We had been searching for Lucy somewhere 30 minutes north of here when a huge, fanged dog had attacked us. As Joe reached for his sword, one of them tore out of his shirt. It was covered in downy white feathers. He'd quickly tried to cover it, putting on his backpack again and saying something about tight muscles. A single feather, loosened by the wind, traveled past my face as we silently continued forward.

"Anyway," Raf continues, "whether or not you believe me, I thought I should tell you. 'And the mother of hell shall appear in your midst, swaddling a babe, and the old angels will meet their end.'"

"When?" I ask.

"Soon. But we all know how relative 'soon' is. Maybe today, maybe 20 years, maybe a couple of decades. Whenever he lets us die, I guess. But most likely, he won't."

And then I was alone with Gabe, who was now snoring in his sleep. I hear the hum of a car engine outside of the building. The headlights are so bright that I wince away. I blink and see that there's a girl sitting inside of it. Her tired eyes look right through me.

As I stand up, my heart thrumming in my chest, I think: Soon. So soon. Too soon. Not soon enough.

I come up to the driver's side. Debris crunches underneath my feet. Everything else around us feels quiet, as if the world had been wrapped in cellophane. Lucy turns toward me and none of the words I could say to her in this moment feel right. I lean in through the window and she pulls my head towards hers so that our foreheads are touching. I listen to her breathe, not closing my eyes. I know that Michael has probably woken up. He's already on his way. But for now, all I want is for us to stay like this.

I hear a small whimper and look down. Her shirt is open, and I see something suckling at her breast. One small furry head wriggles blindly as the other three heads whine, desperate to get ahead of one another. It's the deer fetus I saw outside of the window. I press my face into her head. Her hair smells of salt.

"Lucy," I murmur, and then I feel a small bead of sudden cold inside my chest. There's an angel right behind us.

I reach around my back for my gun, but feel only air. Someone must have taken it while I was out. Michael stares at us, his lance glinting in the sunlight. Instead of a hand, his right arm connects to a red talon, massive and deadly.

I push away from the car. "You have to go—" I say, but then Lucy shushes me.

"Watch," she says. Her voice is deep to the point where I can barely hear it. The fetus shakes inside her shirt.

Michael lets out a scream of pain. Thorns erupt from his body, twisting into the sky. His head is pushed to the side by a growing lump. It dangles from his neck, as an eagle's head bursts forth from the growth. It opens its beak and screeches, a terrible sound that shakes the air around us. I step back as Michael bucks and twists, his spine cracking as it reshapes itself. He's growing larger by the second—six feet, eight feet, twelve—and there's nothing I can do to protect us.

Beside me, Lucy is whispering something. It's not in our language. It's not any human language either. It's something else entirely, darkness that was never supposed to be.

The car door slams against my back. Lucy moves around me, pushing the fetus into my arms. Something light lands on my arm: A glassy, reddened scale.

"Look away now," Lucy says, and her voice is now a growl. Gems shower around us as she continues shedding. Her neck heaves downward. Bones erupt in the space where her head had once been connected and climb on top of each other, forming sharp, ivory branches.

"No," I say.

I think about Isaac. The fragility of his father's heart, his imperfect, innocent faith. I think about how I once believed love could be enough to save someone.

A chain of hardened tissue swings and hits me in the face. The last thing that I see is a flash of red as Lucy lunges toward Michael before plunging both her claws into his eyes.

"It's going to be okay, Zedkiel," I hear Lucy say. I can already feel myself fading. Lucy's is face blurred by the sun as it splinters above us in the sky. It trembles once before breaking completely; large, burning shards falling around the earth, Shrieks erupt from the hospital, and I know that all of the others have begun transforming now, too.

Lucy's tears land on my face and body, huge orbs of black water. I still can't see her face. I wonder how I'll come back. Will I be a demon or a human? Will I be something else entirely? Something like Lucy?

Suddenly, the sky is no longer blank or burning. The clouds part to reveal Israfil, giant, blowing an ivory trumpet in pre-emptive victory. All of God's army follows behind—the angels I had known and those I hadn't, spreading out to fill the sky. I wonder who's replaced me as the other Zedkiel, who is performing my functions. If he's doing a better job than I did.

My lungs can no longer hold air. My eyes lose their form, drip down my caving chest. I want to make sure that the last thing I see in this body, this particular function of my existence, is her. My eye squirms, swivels and finds what it's meant to.

Lucy's fangs are out. She's beautiful. She heaves herself into the sky, leaving me behind to watch. I'm not worried.

Wherever I end up next, she'll find me before God can.

DAMIEN AND MELISSA

Damien decided he would let Melissa try it. After all, it was basically him. At least that's what she told him. And who was he to deny her?

"We haven't been together for almost eight months," Melissa had said on the phone. "I need something here. Something physical."

Damien heard the sound of her chewing. Dill pickle chips? Those were her favorite. He could almost smell them through the phone. *I love you*, Damien thought to himself as she continued chewing. *They are so disgusting, but I love you.*

"Seven and a half, actually," he had said.

"It's the same thing, Damien," she had replied. "Jesus, always so particular."

So now there was a doll/robot thing coming to her doorstep that looked exactly like him. Only with synthetic skin and a synthetic you know what. It was made by this company called PartnerNow!, a startup based in LA, where Melissa was from.

It had been created by this couple who did long distance for five years. Both of the men were tan, mustachioed. Obviously went to the gym. In the video they wore almost identical striped shirts with small hearts on the front, *PartnerNow!* written inside like a promise.

"And then Alex had this idea," the brown-haired guy said, placing his hand over the other's with a soft smile. "What if we *could* be together despite everything?"

"Stop," Alex says, laughing. "It was your idea, too."

The other guy hits him jokingly. It lands with a soft *thwack,* like *this shows that we share a secret life together outside of this video full of tenderness and joy which you cannot even understand but could perhaps one day if you buy our product.*

"Okay, so it was both of our ideas," says the boyfriend, Dimitri. "And a pretty beautiful one at that."

He shifts in his seat, looking directly toward the camera.

"That's when PartnerNow! was born."

PartnerNow! the endscript reads, as the creators, joined by their cyborg counterparts, kiss each other. *Don't let distance keep you from the one you love.*

"This is weird," Damien told Melissa on the phone, watching someone who was either Dimitri or the fake Dimitri tousle the hair of his boyfriend or the pretend boyfriend. "Also, the name is stupid."

"Okay, we don't have to do it. If you really don't want to, we don't have to." She sounded pissed. Lately, that was the only emotion he could get out of her.

"Okay."

"I mean, you obviously don't want to compromise on anything ever. Like that time we were going to get a cat and become farmers in Kentucky."

"That was a while ago."

"*Wow.*"

"What? I'm just telling the truth."

"Forget it. I don't care anymore," she said, and started to cry.

Damien listened to her for a little, trying to figure out what to say before realizing there was only one thing he could say: "Look, Mel, I'm sorry. I'm sorry, okay? We can buy the sex dolls. I mean the robots. I mean the Partners."

After that, he could hear her smiling. "I love you, Big Gulp."

"I love you too," Damien said.

"Thanks for doing this for me."

"Anytime."

They talked for a few minutes about her writing (not going well), her friend Pooja (also not going well), her job at the publishing company (stupid and her boss was stupid and this made her want to die). They said I love you again and then hung up. Damien realized he hadn't even said anything about himself, but even if he had, would she care? Did they even mean it when they said "I love you" anymore, or were they just words they had memorized and repeated to one another for fear the other had forgotten?

Melissa and I used to be happy, Damien thought to himself as he lay in bed. They'd met at a terrible art installation, where videos of the artist's naked body had been projected all over the walls. Damien hadn't been living in the city for very long and was desperate to make friends, so when he had read about it online, he went. When he walked into the room it was quiet, white smoke covering the tile. People moved in small groups of two or three in their winter coats, whispering and nodding at each other importantly. Damien walked up to one of the videos of the artist, where he was sprawled out on the floor like a starfish. His dick was hard. There was nothing interesting at all about him or his body, his stomach that flopped down like a frown. The camera shook and fell off of the tripod before fading into static.

Damien looked around at the rest of the room. A very tall girl was standing beside him, staring at a video in which the artist had stuck his head into the toilet while light streamed in from outside. When the artist dunked his head back into the toilet, causing water to splash all around him, the girl covered her mouth with her hand and turned toward him.

"This sucks," she said, and laughed. Damien laughed with her. The lights moved across her face, leaving flecks of gold inside the brown.

"Right, yeah. It's really bad," he said.

"I loved his earlier work, though. The one with all the stuffed animals."

"Oh, yeah. I loved that one."

"I mean, what he had to say in that one...I thought about it for week!" She spread her arms out wide from beneath her cloak. "'How vast the sorrow of the splintered animal! How victorious are we, its executioner!'"

"Incredible," Damien said. "I sort of thought that he could have gone a bit further with it, though. The stuffed animals."

"I didn't know anything about Welsh underground art until then. Did you?"

"No. It was eye-opening."

"Completely," she said.

There was a second of silence while people mulled

around them toward the exit, still looking thoughtful and serious. Damien looked at his phone; it was almost 11 PM, and the exhibit would be closing soon. Everyone seemed to be leaving, and Damien tried to pretend he needed to be somewhere too.

"Well," he said. "There's somewhere I need to be."

"Then let's go outside until you have to leave."

She grabbed his hand. Her palm was cool and dry.

"Pull it together, man!" she said, laughing as he tripped over a wire in his attempts to keep up.

"Sorry," Damien said, even though he wasn't sure what for.

They got outside and the concrete was damp beneath their feet. She let go of his hand and began walking fast toward the park, eventually breaking into a run. Soon, she was halfway down the sidewalk.

What am I doing? Damien thought, blinking as the rain dripped down his glasses. She deliberately stomped through all the puddles on the crosswalk, and this seemed to Damien like something he should do too. He hit every puddle he could, and by the time they arrived at the park, the rain had stopped. His sneakers were soaked, squelching as they began walking at a normal pace again, the only sound for a while.

"So what is it that you're doing tonight?" she asked.

"I'm...watching a movie. Probably. I don't actually have any plans," he admitted.

"What are you going to watch?" she asked. A gleam of silver shone from her front molar. "And hey, no lying this time," she said, getting so close to Damien's face that he could smell her breath. It was stale and sweet, like the ducks they gave you at Easter.

"Oh."

The girl laughed. She pulled away from him and pulled an umbrella out from her tote. He was too embarrassed to ask why she hadn't pulled it out before. She opened it, moving closer so that he could stand underneath. The rain kept falling, forming a wet halo around them. He still didn't know why they had come to the park.

"I'd never heard about that guy before. And I have no idea what the fuck they do in Wales," she said.

"Why do you run that fast? And why didn't you pull the umbrella out sooner? Why did we come to the park?"

"I'm not that fast. You're just slow. I didn't pull out the umbrella because I didn't want to. We came to the park because I like it. Thank you."

"Okay. Hi, I'm Damien."

"Melissa," she said. "Do you want to go watch a movie?"

"Where?"

"At your place, Damien," she said. She pointed her umbrella at him like a gun and pretended to shoot. "Pew pew."

They got to his place and Melissa asked to take a shower. In addition to her umbrella, she said she also kept an extra pair of clothes, a can of sardines, a pack of cigarettes, a switchblade, a flashlight, and some loose cash on her at all times. Damien told her those were weird things to have and she said she was weird and could she go take a shower now if he didn't mind? He pointed at the room across from his door at the end of the hallway.

As Damien waited for her to finish, he sat on the couch and listened to her sing a song about a tortoise. Her voice was beautiful. When she came back in and Damien could see her fully underneath the lights, he realized that even if she was strange, she was also the most beautiful girl he had ever seen.

She came to sit next to him on the couch. Neither of them moved closer to the other. There was no nervousness between them, he realized. In fact, it felt natural—she should sit on the right side and Damien should sit on the left and that was the way things had always been and should be. Without saying anything, she flicked through the movies on the screen until she chose *The Wonders*. It was Damien's favorite film, but he didn't dare break the silence to tell her. They continued switching off like this, handing the other the remote, only making sounds when they thought something was funny or sad. By the time they got to *Tampopo,* they had already watched 10 movies and it was almost 7 AM. When Melissa began crying in the scene with the raw eggs, Damien didn't understand, though he wanted to. It wasn't just a couple of tears, either: she was sobbing, her head between her knees. It was so loud that he looked around, wondering if one of the neighbors would come knocking soon.

The wailing continued and she began to convulse, all her limbs twitching as if she were a ventriloquist's doll. Damien felt terrified. He paused 120 *Beats per Second* and slid his hand behind her back, rubbing it gently. What should he do now? He cleared his throat and started talking, saying anything that came to mind. He told her that everything was okay and that there was a long future ahead of her and bad things happened sometimes but also good. He told her about the time that he had went to an amusement park and pissed his pants on the water ride so no one could see it. He told her about his friend who was the funniest guy he knew and tried to recreate one joke his friend had where he pretended to be Bob Dylan and was robbing a Walmart, but then Damien started crying, thinking about how he had died two years ago. He put his face between his legs as Melissa rubbed his back and told him her own stories, and they cried some more.

Eventually, both of them stopped crying and started laughing instead. Damien and Melissa hugged each other and he suddenly felt like they had known each other for years. Then she slapped his thigh.

"I like you," Melissa said.

"Me too," Damien said. "I think."

"Now I will pull out my phone and type your number into it. And then we will text each other and make plans for next week. Affirmative?" she said, pretending to be a robot.

"Affirmative."

"Goodbye." She got up, her hands and legs jerking around as she robot-walked to the door. Damien laughed. Her face twitched and Damien pointed at her.

"Hey, you broke character!"

"No. Was— a— glitch — in— my— system—"

"Too late," Damien said, making a fake gun with his fingers. "Pew pew."

She stumbled out of the door, pretending to be mortally wounded. Damien watched as she limped toward the train station, making sure that he wouldn't accuse her of breaking character again.

As Damien closed the door, he felt himself shaking. *I'm not scared*, he told himself, even though he was. Every type of connection back in those days felt like a threat.

Eventually, though, it stopped being so scary in the good way. Two months turned into nine, into a year, and Damien began to wonder if that night had been real, or if things had actually been this way forever. Melissa moved to California and he didn't go with her. At first, they had tried to see each other every three months, but then it seemed like each time they saw each other, all they ever did was fight. Once he had asked her if she only stayed with him out of loneliness and she had slapped him. Both of them stood there unmoving, willing for the other to apologize, but they didn't mention it again. And that was the answer Damien needed.

But that's where they were now; at least they were together. Even if it was only because, as Damien told himself, they were both terrified of the fact that even if they were no longer together, they would both keep existing in the world, and this knowledge was too much to bear.

The delivery came the next day soon after they had signed the contracts and sent in the DNA samples. Damien had gone over the fine print again and again, but he still felt weary. He watched outside the window as two men in a truck backed into his driveway. Or attempted to. What they really did was reverse into the grass, ripping up the earth before backing into the mailbox.

They got out of the truck. One of them pointed to the other and then the other guy pointed back at him and then they were both shouting. The shorter one got back into the truck. He was holding something in his hand that Damien couldn't make out, but then he saw it was a hammer.

"Relax, Marv!" Damien heard the short guy saying before he ran outside. The man raised the hammer and swung at the mailbox. It toppled over. At this point it seemed to occur to them that the person whose front yard they were destroying might be watching. They looked over to where Damien now stood on the porch. He waved.

"Oh, Christ," Marv said.

"Can you stop doing that to my mailbox?" Damien said.

"Was trying to fix it," Marv sniffed, as if he were the one who deserved to be mad in this situation. He dropped the hammer.

The three of them looked at each other.

"I'm sorry," Marv said, waving his hand vaguely toward the yard, "about all of this."

"Can I get a refund?" Damien asked. Now, he was really mad. What was with this attitude? Did this guy know nothing about shame?

"We'll have to see about that," the other guy said. Damien looked at his name tag. "DIMITRI," it read.

"What about the package? Or did you find a way to destroy that, too?" Damien snapped.

"That's very hurtful," Dimitri said.

"Yes, we have the package," Marv said and tugged Dimitri's arm. "C'mon, Dimitri."

The two of them lifted up the back door of the truck. Inside was a box the size of an Ikea shelf, or two Ikea shelves, depending on what size one was thinking of. With surprising grace, Dimitri lifted the box and handed it to Marv.

"Excuse me," Marv said politely, and Damien moved. Marv walked through the open door and placed it on the carpet. Then he walked back out onto the porch and did a weird thing that may have been a curtsy.

"The pleasure is ours," Marv said.

"Is there a number I can call? About the lawn?" Damien asked.

"I tried as hard as I could!" yelled Dimitri, who was sitting in the back of the truck with his head in his hands.

Marv turned back toward Damien. "Sensitive boy, you know," he whispered. "Had a hard childhood and all of that." He pulled out a pen and business card from his shirt pocket.

"Here's the number," Marv said, circling it. "Would appreciate if you could...maybe leave some sort of...mixed review. Mix the good up with the bad."

"Okay," Damien said. Marv put a soiled hand on his shoulder, beaming like Damien was his beloved boy come back from war. He flinched.

"Please don't touch me," Damien said.

"Sorry," Marv said, removing his hand. "Hope everything goes smoothly with that, by the way." He jutted his chin toward the living room. "My boy just got one. Said it's just like the real deal."

"Nobody's like Melissa," Damien said, even though he knew Marv hadn't meant to hurt his feelings and didn't even know who Melissa was. And with that Damien turned around and walked back into his house, slamming the door.

He listened to Marv and Dimitri turn on the engine, idling for a bit before driving away. Or at least that's what he knew he should have been hearing. But in front of Damien was someone who looked just like Melissa. She had evidently shredded her way out of the box, and was now sitting on the living room floor, humming.

Shit, Marv, Damien heard Dimitri yell through the ringing in his ears. *What the fuck did you eat today?* They continued on down the road and were gone.

Damien turned back around and jumped. The girl was standing in front of him, her bruised, skinny knees peeking out from the bottom of her skirt.

The girl moved toward him, and he shivered as its hand moved toward the back of his neck, drawing his face in close to hers. It was Melissa's face, Melissa's mouth curving into a smile. But then she blinked.

Her eyelids had only closed for a beat too long. Maybe less than half a second. But still, it was enough for Damien to notice. She brought up her arms, pointing her fingers at him to form a finger gun. "Pew pew," she said, and laughed. "Why are you acting so weird?"

"Just...a long day at work," Damien said. He noticed the smell of oranges in the air. Just like Melissa's shampoo.

"What are you doing? Do I smell weird or something?" she asked.

Did they like it when you told them the truth? Would they find it offensive? There hadn't been anything in the guidebook about that, but then again, there hadn't been much information at all. He erred on the side of politeness.

"No. No, not at all," Damien said.

She rolled her eyes. A very nervous sort of rain began to fall, sifting through the trees outside. Damien wanted to believe that this was Melissa, that Melissa was just a collection of attributes and behaviors, nothing more. But he could feel his panic dissolving into fear as the cyborg stepped around him toward the kitchen.

"I'm so hungry. Did you even eat anything today at work?" she asked, opening the refrigerator door before he could respond. There was a pause. "Oof. How long has this soup been in here?"

"A couple of days?"

"I'm throwing it out."

As she turned toward the trash can, Damien took the chance to pull his phone out of his pocket and duck into the bathroom, slamming the door behind him as it rang.

After the second ring, Melissa picked up.

"Hey," she said. "Damien and I have been watching a lot of movies together. I mean, sorry. The other Damien."

There was a pause. Damien looked into the bathroom mirror, the black mold forming on its edges framing his face. He realized his lip was bleeding.

"She looks just like you," Damien whispered. "I don't like it."

"That's good, that's good," Melissa said, and Damien wondered if she was even paying attention. "But hey, I'm sorry. That was probably hurtful. I mean, it's not like I don't like watching movies with you. Or maybe I am watching a movie with you, actually. You know?"

"It's okay," Damien said, even though it wasn't. "I'm okay."

"Sorry."

"I'm stupid anyway," Damien said, his voice rising. "I don't know anything about films anymore."

"I don't think that's true."

"I think it's true."

"Stop saying that. You're not stupid."

"Yes, I am. And the other Damien is smarter, and he's cooler, and he's probably a lot more fun to hang out with."

"Well, I did this to strengthen our relationship and it seems like it's not working so maybe I'll just return him and everything can go back to normal which it seems like you want." She said it all really fast and the words seemed to melt together and become one big "I HATE YOU."

"I'm going to go now."

There was a knock on the door.

"Hey, are you okay?" asked the Other Melissa. "You've been in there for a while."

"I'll be right out," Damien said, watching her feet move underneath the door.

"Okay, honey." He listened to her walk back toward the kitchen.

Now it was Melissa's turn to sound hurt.

"She really does sound like me."

"Yeah."

"Well, I guess I'm going to go now."

"Why? What's wrong?"

"Oh, fuck off," Melissa said, and hung up.

Damien picked up his phone.

"What is it, Damien?" In the background he could hear someone with his voice talking, but he tried to ignore it. He wouldn't let her win this one.

"I just wanted to say that it's okay if you don't love me anymore."

"Who said something like that?" Now she was really mad.

"I can tell that you're mad and that you don't love me anymore, and it's okay."

"I'm not doing this right now."

"Okay, then don't. Just hang up the phone."

"I don't want you to call me again if I hang up."

"Okay. Then please just say that you don't love me."

"You're fucking insane, Damien."

"It's okay. It's okay."

She hung up. Damien threw his phone on the ground, where the screen cracked. During their other fights, Melissa was usually the one throwing things, breaking them, but now it was his turn to throw a tantrum. He was allowed that much, right? He was allowed to be angry, wasn't he?

Suddenly, he felt someone's arms around him, telling him that things were okay and that she was here now.

"I'm so horrible," he heard himself crying. In the

distance, an oven timer was going off. "Why am I so horrible? Please, Melissa. Please don't do this to me anymore."

There was a hand smoothing his hair back from his forehead, accompanied by the smell of oranges.

"You don't need to say any of that. You don't ever have to say that."

Damien rolled over on his side, covering his face with his hands. "Really?" he asked, feeling small and stupid.

"Really really."

He closed his eyes. He could believe this was Melissa. This was the real Melissa, and the fake Melissa was the one who had been on the phone who didn't love him. He had made himself believe in plenty of other things before. This wouldn't be hard.

"You're the best thing in the world, Mel," Damien said, more to himself than to the being in the room with him. "You really, really are."

She turned him over and then they were kissing, rolling around on the floor with their hands going up each other's shirts and over their pants. They stumbled up the stairs to his room, where he stroked her beautiful skin and the birthmark he knew so well. Whenever she moaned, Damien remembered how it had been when Melissa and him were first together, how they used to be so good at loving each other. It must've been around two hours that they fucked, and he knew in the back of his mind that the dinner they had been preparing was probably cold. Damien even thought about the person he had called earlier, but as if she could read his mind, Melissa did something that felt so good he came.

Afterwards, Melissa went down and turned off the oven and said that they were lucky the house hadn't burned down. There was smoke everywhere, and she'd raised all the windows to let it out. "That's okay," he said. "It doesn't really matter."

They laid in bed and talked about the things they had done together, like the time they had cut the line at the zoo to see the white tiger, and when the security guard found them, they ran. There was the time they had gone to visit Damien's family, and Melissa had been so nervous that she broke two glasses from gripping them too hard. There was the time they had gone to another exhibit, this time by someone they both knew, and Damien had eaten so much cheese that he farted for hours. They talked about how they used to fall more in love with each other every day, and that their relationship was worth it, and that they were both sorry for how things had been and how much better they would be now that they were together. At some point, Melissa went back down to the kitchen and brought up the burnt potatoes and salmon and limp broccoli and they ate it.

Before they went to sleep, Melissa went to get changed and wash her face. She came back and burrowed her face into Damien's armpit and told him he smelled. The clock read 8:30 PM, but he felt so tired.

"I'll shower in the morning, Mel," Damien said, already feeling himself drifting asleep as he said it. Right before he did, he looked up at her face. There was something like victory in her expression.

Damien had expected for things to feel the same the next day. But when he looked at her face, the small tics were still there: the fact that her mouth opened and closed in a way that was too rhythmic, too practiced of a motion. As she continued talking, Damien nodded, though he wasn't listening to a single word. Had it been designed to know how to make him orgasm in the perfect way too?

The thought made him feel dirty. He felt the urge to shower.

"Sorry," Damien said as Melissa stopped talking, tilting her head in concern. "I should have washed off yesterday."

Melissa nodded. Her lips formed a thin line, but he chose to ignore it, focusing on his breathing as he grabbed a towel and went to the bathroom.

As Damien stepped into the shower, feeling the water trickle down his spine, he thought about the fact that he and Melissa had gotten in one of the same stupid fights they always did. He shook his head, furious with himself. Why couldn't they ever talk about what needed to be talked about for once?

He heard his phone go off and jumped out of the shower, wincing as his knee hit the cabinet. Maybe it was Melissa, texting him to apologize. But as he squinted at the screen, wiping the water off with his towel, he felt his heart drop in disappointment. It was just a message from the postal service telling him that a package had been delivered.

He got dressed and walked out just in time to see Marv driving away. A small box was propped against his front door. Other Melissa hadn't been in the living room when he had walked out, he realized. Damien figured she must have gone back into his bedroom. He would deal with everything later.

He walked back inside, tearing the package open to reveal a small blue wristband inside. It resembled a smart watch, nestled inside pink styrofoam. Underneath was a small card with a message written in swirly font.

Thank you for using PartnerNow! We're so happy that you chose us, and congratulations on beginning your journey. We know that the first day may be difficult for some, but relax. We've got you covered. Enclosed inside this box is your PartnerPizzaz, designed to collect that last bit of information and body language from you so that your partner can truly feel they're spending time with the one they love. The best part? It's helping your partner feel the same, too! We're doing everything we can to ensure that you two can enjoy your relationship, even when you're apart. And we've added some of our signature flair—just as a bonus to show off to your friends.

;)

PartnerNow

He flipped it over to the back to read the directions. "Snap it on and go!" it read. "We recommend that you do this on your second day, as soon as you receive it. After a week, you're safe to remove it (but keep it on if you want to show it off!)"

It was so cold inside. Damien shivered, turning the thermostat up to 75. He thought about what Mel had said. That she was doing this for them. For Damien. The wristband had a stupid plastic diamond glued on each side, what he presumed they meant by "flair." But whatever. If nothing else, this could be his only way of proving to her that he still cared.

It flickered as he put it on, the white letters telling him the process had begun. He clicked the button on the side to dim it. His eyes hurt. He was still so tired.

Damien headed back to his room. All of the lights were off, but he could still make out a Melissa-shaped lump beneath the covers. He sighed. If nothing else, at least this version was consistent—any time Melissa was hurt or wanted to signal that she was angry, she would pretend to be asleep, not responding to anything he said until she decided that he had been punished enough. The Partner-Pizzaz flickered again. Damien tried to dim it again, but it remained bright as ever, the only light inside the room.

"Stupid fucking thing," Damien muttered to himself. "At least make your shit work right."

He considered briefly if he should take it off. Maybe it would be for the best.

But before he could do so, the Other Melissa turned around, turning the lights on.

"I was wondering when you'd get back," she said, yawning. "I've been so sleepy."

There was something different about her voice now. It was smoother, clearer, as if someone had sanded down any of the unevenness it had before. She stretched, her shoulders circling back in one fluid motion. Even her armpits seemed to have taken on a more lifelike quality, fine black hair barely visible in the light.

She reached toward his hand and looked at the wristband.

"What's this?" she asked, giggling. "Some stupid thing Kelechi gave you?"

Kelechi was Damien's best friend—an artist who, as of recent, had taken to designing jewelry and would give the ones that didn't turn out so well to Damien as a gift. So far, Damien had received a slightly dented ring, a necklace carved in the shape of a crane, its wings reaching around either side of his neck.

Why are you acting like you don't know what it is? Damien wanted to ask her, but he kept his mouth shut as she continued examining it. Maybe they didn't give the cyborgs much information about how it all worked either—she seemed genuinely confused, raising her head to ask him again if this was another one of Kelechi's creations.

"Yeah," Damien said, surprised at how effortlessly the lie rolled off of his tongue. "He gave it to me the other week."

"It's nice of you to wear it. Remember to keep it on when we see him next week."

Had he made plans to see Kelechi? Damien racked his brain. They saw each other often, almost every other day, so it seemed plausible. He had already told Kelechi about the entire ordeal, though Kelechi had seemed uncomfortable about it.

"I don't know, man," Kelechi had shrugged as they sat in his living room, passing the joint between them. He exhaled some smoke from the corner of his mouth. "I don't trust it. But that's just me." Kelechi wasn't usually one to broach emotional topics, but not because he was incapable of it. Damien had seen him coach many of his other friends through difficulties before, which meant that Kelechi knew that Damien couldn't handle too much opening at once.

"Yeah," Damien had said. "Yeah."

Kelechi looked at him with something like pity, and then grabbed Damien's hand, placing the crane necklace into his palm.

"You promise me you'll let me know if something happens, yeah?"

"Yeah." He'd said, and tried not to cry as he placed it inside his pocket, reaching out to grab the joint.

Now, Damien sat on the bed, where had he put that necklace afterward? The exhaustion swept over his body.

"If you need to sleep, go ahead. I'll make something for

lunch." Melissa kissed him and he smiled, head already resting against the pillow.

"Don't know why I'm so tired," he murmured.

Melissa laughed. "Oh, you know why."

"Guess so," he heard himself say. And then he slept, dreaming of things that didn't make sense: standing on warm sand at the beach, completely naked, an orange bouquet of flowers growing from the center of his body, roses and petunias and hyacinths falling all around him as he watched Melissa jump into the ocean, laughing as her head slipped off her neck.

Sometimes, he forgets the details: Had two of her friends dropped her off? Or had he met her at the airport? She hadn't brought any of her belongings from California, but when he asked her why, she said they had gone over this.

"I'm all about minimalism now," she said. "Which is why we're also getting rid of *this*," she said, brandishing a small, golden koi model at him.

They were cleaning the house, as they always did on Saturdays now. It was different from the way they used to live, laundry strewn around the house, bent books stacked wherever the owner had abandoned them: the bathroom, the sticky kitchen table. Each time they got rid of something, he would feel lighter, just like Melissa said. But some things he felt particularly attached to. Like the koi.

"You gave me that for our first anniversary," he said, but Melissa was already shaking her head, placing it inside of the trash bag.

"I'll get you something else. Something better. You never cared much about that thing anyway. Look, it had dust all over it," she said, spreading out her hands to reveal grey fingertips.

Damien nodded. It had been six months now since she had come back, and they never fought any more. It was wonderful. And in the time she'd been away, she'd picked up so many new things, skills that made their lives easier: Cleaning and getting rid of unnecessary objects was only one of them. Another one was that they spent a lot more time with just each other. This was because people, along with objects, could also be carriers of negative energy. Kelechi being one of them. The last time they had seen him for coffee, he seemed uncomfortable. He kept looking at Melissa, staring at her either with anger or sadness, Damien couldn't tell. He wanted to text Kelechi afterwards, ask if he was doing okay, but Melissa had told him that it was awful to even consider talking to someone who obviously didn't like her anymore, why would Damien want to continue being friends with someone who hated her? So he said, okay. He would block Kelechi. And after that, he found he didn't even miss him, though this fact made him sad. He wondered if they had really been as close as he'd once imagined.

There was also another time that had brought on a potential fight, but it had been easy enough to deal with. They had gone to ride a shitty roller coaster on the boardwalk together, where Damien lost his phone. Mel finally found it after calling it for what felt like hours. Along with her calls, however, he noticed a slew of notifications from a different number—Mel's old one from before she changed it back to this area code. He briefly looked through the texts out of curiosity and felt panicked. All of them were cries for help— "I love you," read one, "I'm so scared." He thought he might have even seen his name, but then

Melissa had accused him of cheating on her and screamed at him on the boardwalk in front of everyone. She had grabbed his phone and blocked that number, too. He felt like saying that maybe the person was in danger, but at that point, he was too embarrassed to do anything. Everyone kept staring as they left. By the time they had gotten back home, he comforted himself by saying it wasn't really his problem anyway. Hopefully, it had been dealt with.

This week, Damien and Mel were going to an exhibit at the same spot where they first met. The artist had set up the space to look like a factory, and Damien was really excited—he actually knew the artist this time, but Melissa seemed unhappy. She said that his view of technology and mechanics seemed insidious. "That's the entire point," Damien had said when she first brought it up. "His work focuses on the nature of mass surveillance and the misuse of data by the government to inform a heavier police presence in certain neighborhoods." Since when had she developed such strange political views? Was she a libertarian now or something?

"We'll talk about it later," Melissa said, grabbing the keys from the hook. Her face was pinched. "I'm going to go get some groceries."

After he heard the car leave from the driveway, Damien went through his old clothes to see if he could drop off anything at the thrift shop. He threw a couple of shirts, a coat, and some beanies in a bag, feeling upset about how the conversation had gone, wondering if he had been in the wrong. A striped flannel fluttered out from beneath a stack of Melissa's sweaters. It was one of his favorites, and he hadn't seen it for over a year. Delighted, he shrugged it on, relishing the softness of the fabric slipping over his arms. A slip of paper fell out of his front pocket, and he bent over to pick it up.

DIMITRI
PARTNER 2.0
1-800-0101

The idiot who messed up my yard, Damien thought. Then he froze. Had that been the same day Melissa had come back? The more he tried to remember, the more frustrated he became: his mind was a maze of static, and no matter where he turned, he found another dead end just before he could arrive at the memory.

His hands trembled as he called the number on the card. It rang once before going to voicemail. Damien immediately called again, trying to ignore the mounting anxiety building in his stomach telling him that if Melissa came back and saw what he was doing, something very bad would happen.

He ran outside onto the sidewalk, not stopping until he was outside of the school a couple blocks from his building. Children walked by holding their parents' hands, laughing and pointing at the snow, their breaths white and visible in the air. Suddenly, he felt so lonely. How long had it been since he felt that safe? How long had it been since he was excited to tell someone about how his day had gone? Someone besides Melissa?

Finally, someone picked up.

"Hello?" The voice on the other end yawned.

"Hi, yes. This is Damien. We met around a year ago. Do you remember me?"

"Oh, yeah, yeah," Dimitri said. There was a creaking

noise as Dimitri sat up in bed. "I'm still super sorry about the yard."

"That's okay," Damien said, gripping the phone so hard that his knuckles turned white. "I know...I know that this is going to sound like a stupid question, but could you tell me what you were there for?"

Dimitri grew quiet. "Oh, Christ," he whispered. "Not again."

"What do you mean, not again?" Damien was yelling now, and the parents quickly ushered their children along as he stood in the middle of the sidewalk. "What do you mean?"

"There's nothing I can do but say I'm sorry. Happened to my buddy, too."

"What do you mean?" Damien asked for a third time. Did he even want to know? His mind kept zapping each time another image passed through. Melissa eating dill pickle chips. Melissa talking to him on the couch. Melissa and him on the floor. Who had called him that night?

"Look, I'm just a contractor, okay? I didn't have anything to do with that stuff. If you want any answers, well. Have you looked at the news recently?"

Damien hung up. It had in fact been a long time since he had looked at the news, for fear that he may come across something sad that would impart its negative energies onto him. But that was also Melissa's fear, something else that wasn't his. As he went to open the news app, he saw a text from Melissa pop up. There was no message, rather, she had dropped a pin to her location. She wasn't anywhere near the grocery store, despite having only left ten minutes ago. In fact, she was headed directly back toward him.

Damien ran, his muscles remembering the years he had

spent on the track team back in high school. Back then, he had been able to run a mile in 5.4 minutes, loving how blurred the world around him became as his feet pounded against the ground. He used to believe in himself, he remembered as he turned the corner to where the public library was, flying through the automatic doors. He had lost to Melissa that day when they had first met because he no longer believed in himself, not because he was slow. He had never told her that.

Damien slowed down as he reached the computers, his breath rattling in his chest as he sat down and logged on. He turned off the location on his phone, but he was sure that Melissa would be here regardless, and soon.

PARTNER 2.0, he typed, and clicked the search button.

Alan Guo, age 35, and Ihan Rojas, age 36, will stand trial Tuesday on charges of drug manufacturing and cultivation, extortion, identity theft, and homicide in relation to their former company, Partner 2.0.

More and more people were becoming accustomed to the strange humanoid figures with translucent skin frequenting coffee shops or shopping for cereal in the grocery store when they first began appearing in 2019. Though it felt discomforting at first, Tim Farrorway, a manager of a diner in Memphis, Tennessee, said that he felt better knowing that some people would be feeling a little less lonely with their new cyborg partners provided to them by PartnerNow! "I thought that it was a good thing," Farroway said to reporters on Wednesday. "I mean, sure, I was worried that they would end up taking our jobs away, but the president said that we wouldn't need to worry about that. And technology takes some getting used to. They were here to help us out during a particularly lonely time in history...most young people are dating people over the computer and stuff like that. And I figured well, if the government is saying that it's a way to encourage the young men in this country to keep going, that they're not alone, I could get used to the idea that my friends are all out there getting it on with robots."

Dimitri Pengovich, a delivery contractor who worked for PartnerNow! for around six months before quitting, said he felt ambivalent. "It was a job. They paid me a lousy $10/hour, not even enough to cover gas money. Many of my friends were signing up for the service too, and they seemed happy about it. I didn't like the idea of hauling around things that could come to life at any point, though. Gave me the creeps. I quit as soon as I could." Pengovich now works for a food delivery service, where he makes $14/hour. "It's all shit. At the end of the day, all these places are just corrupt. But me? I don't have a choice. I have to make an earning somewhere."

Caught up in their own lives and jobs, Pengovich and Farroway wouldn't begin noticing the differences in their friends' behaviors until much later. But for Cathy Jun, she caught on almost immediately. Two weeks after her nephew Stanley Hong had opted into PartnerNow's! services, she went to visit him and see what this new cyborg was like. To her horror, she found that Hong showed no recognition of her when she stepped through the door. Even more horrifying was the fact that the strange, mannequin-like woman who bore a crude resemblance to Hong's partner, who Cathy had known for ten years since the couple first began dating, kept assuring Cathy that everything was fine despite the fact that Hong seemed to be in an acute state of stress and paranoia. Cathy tried to move toward Hong, but the woman quickly blocked Cathy from reaching him, eventually shoving her out the door as Hong continued muttering to himself and pulling at the strange wristband on his arm, showing no signs of recognizing his beloved aunt. The next day, when Cathy attempted to visit Hong's home again, she found it empty.

"We went from calling every week for two years to nothing...I called and called his phone, but it seemed as if it had been changed. I thought to myself, I have to find him. I have to," Cathy said to reporters last week as she broke down on stage at a recent press conference.

Cathy took to social media afterward, asking others about their experiences with the company. "PartnerNow! has stolen my nephew from me," she said in a now-deleted post. "I am convinced that this company is nothing but pure evil. Has this happened to anyone else? Please DM me, I am so afraid." She received thousands of replies in return, with people reporting similar interactions with their loved ones. For a while, Cathy thought that perhaps this would be enough evidence to make PartnerNow! come clean, but her social media account was taken down three hours later, and all the negative posts about PartnerNow! that people had made following Cathy's tweet were now nowhere to be found. "It was at that point that I knew something was wrong...very, very wrong."

Cathy started to protest outside of their headquarters all by herself, but soon, many came to join her, each demanding that PartnerNow! revert their loved ones back to their normal states. The protests drew national attention in September of 2020, inciting the first round of investigations.

How it works

The cyborgs created by PartnerNow! would orally administer a drug known as Fexopoline to those they were assigned to on the first day of arrival. Fexopoline, which promotes pair bonding and increases suggestibility, works in tandem with a methadone type drug called Damphine, injected into the victims' bloodstreams via a small blue wristband, causing acute memory loss. Together, the drugs work quickly to enter the bodies of the victims and travel up to the amygdala, hippocampus, and neocortex, absorbing memories and personality traits that the cyborgs could then easily access as soon as all of the information had been extracted. Over time, the same parts of the brain that had initially been stolen from begin to break down. This process could be repeated as many times as necessary, which has resulted in many victims losing up to five years of memories. So far, it seems as if these memories cannot be recovered, but scientists say that there may be some hope in time.

Over 6,000 victims have been identified at this time, though the total number is still unknown. Teams of data scientists, armed with special weapons used to stun the cyborgs before disassembly, have been working alongside trauma-informed psychologists across the country to aid victims in what is sure to be a long road to recovery.

"It is very important that victims are given this information in a slow, careful manner, so as not to cause complete mental breakdown," Dr. Gerard, one of the psychologists currently involved in the investigations warns. "While some of them may have lost their memories entirely, those who are in the earlier stages and just beginning to suspect that something is happening should not be overwhelmed with all of this at once."

Early Beginnings

Guo and Rojas were film students in their 20's when they befriended a woman named Melissa Ahuja. The three instantly became close, with Ahuja playing a role in many of Guo and Rojas' experimental films, appearing many times in the role of "S," a woman who enjoyed sadism and was often shown in various scenes in rope bondage. Ahuja eventually broke ties with the two, claiming that she was drugged and hypnotized on multiple occasions, but dropped her charges once they settled on a 1 million dollar lawsuit.

Ahuja seemed to enjoy a relatively normal life after this —that is, until the long-term effects of the drugs began to take effect. Ahuja has attested from her current place of residence in an intensive psychiatric care clinic that she would often experience intense episodes of depersonalization and psychosis. Ahuja claims that she had "lost any form of autonomy" in early 2020, causing her to agree to be a part of Guo and Rojas' startup. Ahuja was one of the first people to begin recruiting people to sign up for the service, including her partner, Damien Okamoto. Though Ahuja fought as hard as she could against the mind control Guo and Rojas had inflicted upon her, she says that the most she could manage was "Five minutes of lucidity a week. Seven, if I forced myself to bear the pain." During those precious moments, she attempted to contact the people she knew had signed up for the service, including Okamoto. To her dismay, no one responded.

Though Ahuja has been kept relatively stable since entering into psychiatric care, she says that she managed to destroy the counterpart of her partner, Damien Okamoto, during a rare ten minutes of lucidity before escaping from their shared home. When police arrived on the scene, they found that the cyborg did not, in fact, resemble Okamoto at all. Cyborgs, to the normal person who has not been administered Fexopoline and Damphamine, are very crude replications of their human alters. Their translucent skin and jerky, unnatural movements are immediately noticeable to any onlookers, but victims cannot see any disparities between the cyborgs and their real partners. It is a testament to Ahuja's strength that she was able to fight off the effects of the two drugs at all, not to mention the ones that had continuously destroyed her over the years during her friendships with Guo and Rojas.

Ahuja is still worried about her partner, Damien Okamoto, as she is afraid that her own counterpart is most likely highly dangerous, possibly due to Guo and Rojas' preemptively adding on stronger security components should Okamoto ever come to his senses. "They are completely obsessed with me...they would do anything, anything to keep me from happiness. They're f-ing monsters. They loved seeing me alone in this world, loved seeing how many people they could distance me from. I never...I never told Damien. He was the only person who never left me. Maybe he would hate me for keeping it a secret for so long, I guess is what I thought. I don't know what it is about him, but when we were together, I felt safe. Even when those horrible things inside of me popped back up, the violent parts, the...evil parts, he wouldn't leave. I knew they were monitoring us. We'd passed by them twice on the street in a year, but they couldn't do anything. Damien would have protected me, always."

Authorities say that this has been an especially difficult case to handle, as even though they have been monitoring patterns of Ahuja's counterpart's behavior for some time now, they were recently recognized by the cyborg and are now unsure if intervention will result in placing Okamoto in more danger. Kelechi Nwaike, a long-time friend of Okamoto's, reported to authorities several months ago that Okamoto was "completely gone." Though he made several attempts to save Okamoto since finding out the horrible news, even going so far as to meet the cyborg and Okamoto together, he found that getting through was impossible. The cyborg controlled every aspect of his life. "I just want my friend back," he says, his head low. "If he ever manages to see this, I want him to know that I loved him. That the real Melissa loves him. And everything is going to be okay." Nwaike regularly visits Ahuja at the hospital, and the two have created a support group for victims' loved ones.

If you know of someone who may have....

Damien scrolled back up and looked at the picture of Melissa they had posted in the article. For a moment, he felt betrayed—not because she hadn't told him about what happened, but because he had no idea who the Melissa in this photo was; the young, skinny girl with poorly bleached hair wearing pink lingerie, her form silhouetted against the dark.

He heard the person at the front desk welcome someone, shortly followed by a scream. Maybe it was her, or the people who were supposedly coming to save him.

Damien didn't look up as he felt a cold hand touch his shoulder, its nails sinking into his skin. He wanted to think of one memory he could remain sure of, even if all the other ones would disappear. He closed his eyes as the library patrons screamed louder, unable to see the three men tackling the translucent woman and plunging a syringe into her stomach, black, worm-like wires squirming out of her skin and onto the floor, where they kicked about violently before dying.

That time she had slapped him, he had held her hand against his face, not allowing her to draw away even as she sobbed. They had stayed there like that for five minutes, maybe even more. He had forgotten that later that night, she had tapped him on the shoulder like a timid child and offered him something.

"What is it?" Damien had asked as he looked at the small, chipped rock laying in her palm.

"It's a rock," Melissa had said, not looking at him as she spoke. "I got it from Alaska. It's really special to me."

What he should have done was taken it, told her how much it meant to him. He should have commented on the way that it sparkled underneath the kitchen light, how cool it felt against his skin. But instead he had thrown it across the tile so that it shattered in two.

"I don't fucking care," Damien had said and trudged up the stairs, the shame already threading itself around his heart. Melissa had gone to sleep at a friend's house that night. He felt too terrible to call her.

The next day they had pretended like everything was normal, and though he looked for it, the rock wasn't anywhere. Melissa must have taken it and put it away somewhere, this rock that was so special to her for reasons he would now probably never know.

Perhaps this was a bad memory to keep with him,

Damien thought to himself as he was carried out of the library by two large men, the figure who was supposed to be Melissa writhing on the floor as the other men pinned it to the ground. Perhaps he should try harder to think of a good one, one where he and Melissa had been happy. They lifted him into the truck but paused as they saw him shake his head against the thought.

"Are you alright?" The larger man asked, concerned.

Damien nodded and the two men looked at each other before getting into the front. Outside, the sidewalks and grass were still cloaked in snow, the familiar now buried underneath white frost. The truck lurched and Damien thought to himself again that there was so much about Melissa that he never understood. To a certain extent, she had resisted his understanding, and the most he could do now was respect that. To love in full this person he had never really known.

They passed by a house, where ice-covered flowers stood stiff inside the dirt. A single orange geranium peeked its head out from underneath the white crust, though it remained unseen.

THE RABBIT GOD

1. *Fate is predictable because it is lonely.*
2. *What is stolen by fate can be begged or borrowed back.*
3. *There is little difference between a boy and a god and a ghost.*
4. *By the end of my story, you will have forgotten how it goes.*

"I got a job," I told my father at dinner. On the table, my mother placed plate after plate of dumplings and beef, greens gleaming with oil, perfectly rounded bowls of rice in front of us. Even six people couldn't finish all this food. Why cook such extravagant meals that no one would eat? To make up for the discomfort of pretending we were a family?

Instead of answering, Father began poaching different items with his chopsticks, placing them into his bowl. My mother gave me a pale smile. For once, I wish she'd be brave.

"Where's the job?" she asked.

"At a mall. I'll be working as a security guard."

My mother nodded, her gaze already diverted elsewhere. Her eyes were at once empty and startlingly large.

"Why don't you have any friends?" Father asked, and my mother ducked into the kitchen to get tea, not wanting to listen.

"I do," I said. "I hang out with—"

"No," he said, cutting me off. He ate like an animal: without thought or pause. "Male friends. Male. Not girls."

Mother slipped back in quietly. She began pouring tea into our cups. Bits of her scalp showed through her thinning hair.

"Here you are," my mother said. She turned toward me, smiling. "Where's the job?"

"I told you already. At the mall."

"Is it true?" she asked.

"Yes? I start tomorrow."

My father finished eating, leaving his dishes on the table. He went up the stairs. The sounds of the radio floated down toward us.

"Well isn't that nice," my mother said.

Both of us sat there, staring at the leftover meal, already growing cold. *Is it true?* kept echoing through my head. She hadn't been asking about the job.

My boss was a thin man with a tanned face. His khaki uniform made him look like a soldier. He lit a cigarette and nodded for me to take one, but I shook my head. He shrugged.

"It's not hard," he said. People were trickling in outside of the room: entire swarms of them, pawing through t-shirts and vinyl purses, paper fans, plastic cars and trains, rows of golden jewelry. Workers belted at them about the low prices, the high qualities of their items. They were hollow, too, but more sympathetic. I felt how they felt; or at least something similar. "Just go through the rooms to make sure there's no homeless guys or thieves or whatever."

There was a flashlight and a set of keys on a huge red ring, as well as my own uniform placed on the table next to him.

"You can carry this, too, if you want," he said. He handed me a metal rod with a clip on the end, where it could attach to my pants. His hand slid across mine and paused. Our fingertips met for two or three seconds, and he was looking at me for the first time.

I drew my hand back, panicked. "What keys are these?" The room was so small. I could smell the cologne on his skin, the gel in his hair.

He sucked his teeth. Through the smoke, his disappointed face looked exactly like my father's. "Figure it out."

It was darker than I'd expected. Shirts fluttered on metal racks, like ghosts without frames. Every time I shined the flashlight into a room, I imagined that now would be when I'd see them: the lovers, their bodies forming into one another's; a man with a vendetta who would plunge a knife into my back. Humidity clung to my face as I searched for them. But there was never anything but my own shadow, grotesque and overgrown, hunting me through the corridors.

After an hour or so, I stopped being scared. At one of the women's clothing stores, I saw a row of purple dresses, all different from each other. A tight bodycon dress for clubbing, a thin cotton shirt dress, an A-line dress, perfect for an office worker. On the mannequin was a beautiful lilac dress with ruffle details, its skirts layered. Satin florals decorated the fabric.

Is it true? My mother had said. I thought about the boys at school, their cruel faces, the way they ran away from me in pretend fright as we changed for gym class. I thought about my boss with the tanned, chiseled face. The flowers on the lilac dress glistened as I reached out for it and pulled it over my head. It fell with ease over my starched uniform, landing just above my knees.

I kept walking through the rooms, but I felt energized now in my fear. The lilac dress didn't judge me, it simply moved along with me, floating around my body as we continued on our search. I walked up the stairs to the third floor. Foliage coiled around the pillars like emerald snakes. The leaves appeared wet, hungry.

Laughter tumbled down from the floor above me, like an avalanche of rushing snow. I screamed, falling to the floor, holding the flashlight in both hands like a weapon. The yellow light whipped around the darkness, finding nothing. The laughter echoed louder, but there was nothing cruel about it. It was happy, innocent, like a child's.

And then it stopped. I grabbed the skirts around me, clenching it in my fists.

"Who's there?" I said. "Who's there?"

Shenhang Hu
March 15, 1990

I talked to that guy today. The one who's always crying. It's because Xiao Feng's always fucking with him. The kid's an easy target. They've taken his gym pants at least five times this month. Instead of doing anything, he'll just sit there and wrap himself up in a little ball as they all throw water bottles and towels at him. He's always wearing goofy underwear. Today, it had little cute cartoon rabbits on it. You'd think after all of this he'd just buy new briefs, right? It's a little pathetic.

I stayed around until they all were gone and went up to him. *Hi*, I said, but he didn't move. So I walked over to the other end of the bench. *I'm not gonna hurt you, alright?* I tried to be funny about it, flinging my hands up in the air. Still nothing. So I told him that they used to do the same stuff to me, and that's when he looked up. God, he's beautiful. He has this face like tempered glass. Ornamental. I can't stop thinking about it. Since he'd been crying, it was flushed pink. Between his stupid briefs and the look on his face, I kept thinking about something I read in a book once: rabbits, when placed on their backs, freeze up. They can't move or fight back, so it just looks like they're resting. Meanwhile, they're scared shitless. It's considered animal cruelty, but people still do it to their pet rabbits all the time. Maybe they know or maybe they don't. It doesn't really matter, does it?

Suddenly, he seemed embarrassed about being naked, or semi-naked. I reached into my bag and gave him a pair of extra pants I had. I turned away as he changed. I do admit I looked back just once, and he has these long legs, strong yet thin, like a dancer's. *Thanks*, he mumbled. He was shaking. I told him to not mention it.

In the spring, all these little pink flowers come blushing up from the pockets of earth. I started walking toward the bike rack, but then I realized he wasn't beside me anymore. When I looked back, I saw him doing the strangest thing.

Even though it was impossible, he was trying to step around every little pink flower on the ground. It would've taken him an hour at least to get through without crushing one. But he was dancing around them, almost losing his balance, attempting it anyway. I fell in love with him instantly.

March 16, 1991

He wasn't in gym class today. Xiao Feng and his friends seemed disappointed, deflated. Everything felt so boring without him. I biked home feeling like maybe it was my fault, like I'd scared him away. But then I saw a boy walking along the side of the road.

Hey, I called out, and he turned around. That same stunned look on his face. I'm always trying to look braver than I actually am. Last night, actually, I wrote him a poem. I don't think it was any good, now that I think about it. I'm embarrassed I even gave it to him. But when I took it out of my bag, he read it hungrily, quickly, and I could see his lips moving, making out some of the words under his breath. I almost fainted.

After he was done, he folded it carefully and placed it inside of his pocket. He smiled. But his smile was the saddest thing I'd ever seen. I told him that he could come back to my place, if he wanted. That my mom wasn't ever home. He didn't nod or anything, but he still followed me back home. then he sat perched on the corner of my bed until I pushed him backward. I think he's a virgin, he wasn't very good in bed at first, but after a while, he got the hang of it. We went at it for at least two hours, I think, and then he told me he had to go.

I just remembered something. He didn't tell me anything about what he thought about my poem. I don't know how to feel about that. Should I ask him? I don't know. I guess it doesn't really matter. He's still got the most beautiful mouth I've ever seen.

The laughter stopped. I ran down the stairs, but upon reaching the second floor, I saw that the shops kept repeating themselves. I wasn't moving at all.

I heard a whistle. Dangling from the balcony, one arm curled around a banister, was a boy. I could tell from his voice he was smiling as he dropped from the balcony. My flashlight blinked in and out a few feet away from me, where I'd dropped it. The flickering lights distorted his movements, making him appear as if we were in a horrific stop motion animation.

I closed my eyes, but I felt his breath everywhere: even, calm. He grabbed my cheek with cold hands, turning me toward him, but I didn't look up. I couldn't.

The fingers drummed against my skin, familiar and distressing. "Oh, come on. Is that any way to treat a dead man?" He said. "Look at you. Playing dress-up now?"

He fingered the sheer sleeve of my dress. "Look at me." It was a command.

I'd always hated how effortless everything was for him. His nonchalant beauty, so perfect it seemed almost false, like a whisper of dew. The perfect curls of his eyelashes dragged me downwards, down toward the memories I couldn't see without screaming.

He smiled and began walking toward the exit, where no light awaited us. There would be people outside, there always were, but none of them would stop us. His footsteps made no sound. I followed. Out of guilt, maybe. Or perhaps it was hope, a stupid wish for forgiveness. I didn't ask where we were going.

Shenghang Hu
March 15, 1992

My mom figured it out. Or as she put it, she can tell that "I've found someone special." She's always tired when she gets home from work, I didn't think she noticed. She was painting her nails in the living room and stopped me. As a child, I cried whenever she wasn't around. Now that she's gone so much, I had to get used to it. But I still miss her so much. She asked me where I was yesterday night. *Out with a friend,* I told her. *A friend, huh?* I said yes. She asked if I was happy. I want my mom to think I'm happy, always, all the time. I don't want her to ever know I'm miserable. So I told her yes, I was. When she asked if I'd ever bring him around, I told her I didn't think so. She got quiet after that. Then she told me about this rabbit that she sees now whenever she leaves the house. She said it doesn't move, it just sits there on the grass. She wanted to pet it but she felt like that was a bad thing to do. I wonder if I'm doing a bad thing, too, but I'm the rabbit. Not him.

Then she told me there was this couple she cleaned houses for sometimes. She doesn't like to speak badly of people, but she said that the wife "wasn't all there," and that they were not nice people. As I walked out of the house, she told me that he went to my school, and that if I saw him around, I should make sure he's doing okay.

The funny thing is that he's doing fine; I'm the one who's suffering. It was raining tonight when I walked into the forest. He kissed me, but it was like he was so far away from me, I hardly felt his lips. I told him I loved him, but he just kissed me again. I feel so stupid every time I say that, so pathetic, but I keep hoping that one day he'll say it back.

He never speaks to me at school. If I try, he'll get angry. It hurts sometimes to see him, this person who I can only know at certain times, touch at certain times. And I'm a coward; I never bring it up. If I tried, then maybe he wouldn't talk to me anymore. Sometimes, I forget that I was the one who comforted him that day. I liked it better when it was the other way around; when he was the weak one, the fucked up one, the one who needed me. Is that evil to say? And when he apologizes, the apology is netted in a thing like guilt. I feel like I should pry into its meaning, but who knows what would happen if I did.

We sat there, huddled under a tree for a while, before I told him that he could go; I didn't mind. But he said that it was okay. That he wanted to stay there with me, and that he was sorry.

What is he sorry for? The fact that he wants me? The fact that he fucks me? Is he sorry that he's all friendly with those assholes who tormented him now, that he stands and watches as they throw their bags at me? Is he sorry that he's hit me twice now, right after I reach for him on the other side of a motel bed? I never know when he'll be in the mood to like me, be kind to me, or when he'll be in the mood to pretend that I'm dead or, as he's put it, "different than him."

But we're not different, we're the same. He's the guy who wore the stupid briefs and I'm the guy who took them off later that day in my bedroom, placed his dick in my mouth as he clenched the back of my head. I don't think I'm asking for too much but now I can't even write his name in this journal any more. It feels like I'm not allowed to say it.

March 20, 1992

He always watches for people we might know, even when it's night outside. Always nervous that someone will see us and they'll start on him again instead. Since when did I become so okay with being treated like this? What did this guy do to my head?

We reached this old noodle shop, one that's been around for ages. Normally, we never eat meals together in public. If we eat, it's takeout, and we eat it in the park or forest or at my house when my mom's at work. But then he said: *Are you hungry? I'll buy us food.*

I was shocked. Or terrified, or elated, maybe all of those things. I nodded. In that moment, he looked nervous and twitchy like the first week we started seeing each other. Wanting for me to like him, wanting to impress me. He'd shown me a scar on his stomach from a surgery he'd gotten as a kid. *Touch it,* he'd said, the third time we'd fucked. But when I touched it, it felt like anything. Like it could've been anyone else's skin.

When we walked inside the noodle shop, there was a man in the back twisting noodles with his hands, an infinite loop of white. The place was basically empty. We walked to the back and sat down at this cracked vinyl booth. He ordered us two bowls of mi sua boy (he had sad eyes, eyes like my own). The server's hands shook. I felt bad. Maybe the kid was like us. No, that's not accurate. Maybe the kid was like him.

I sat and ate my noodles for a while until I heard him say, *Do they taste good?* His voice was softer than it'd been in weeks. I wanted to weep. For some reason, I felt like throttling him. In my mind a million possibilities played out: he'd found someone else, that's why he'd asked me to come here, that's why he's being nice. I'm allowed to be paranoid, I think. It's the least he can afford me.

But right before I could say anything, demand an answer, he placed something on the table wrapped in this beautiful pink and gold paper. The note's right beside me now, I haven't gotten the nerve to throw it out yet: "Happy Anniversary." It all makes me feel so stupid. Not because I'd doubted him, but because I'm still in love with him.

He asked if I thought he'd forgotten. I snapped at him, saying that he'd never told us that we were even dating. *Lower your voice,* he'd hissed. But he tried to hold my hand, curling it over mine. It all felt so forced. The server was still watching us, but from a little bit away, pretending to be wiping a cup. When he met my eyes, he scurried into a corner, wiping it harder.

I'm sorry. Go ahead and open it, he said. When I ripped open the paper, I saw a grey cover with a faint gold title: *The Han Garden Collection.* It's a poetry anthology edited by Bian Zhillin, that genius Symbolist poet who I love and have talked about so much to him, but I never imagined he was actually listening. More and more these days, I talked just to hear myself speak, to know that I'm still alive.

First edition, too, he said, raising an eyebrow. His face was flushed red from the steam. *He burped. Go ahead, why don't you choose a poem? Read it out loud.*

I flipped through the table of contents until I found one by Bian Zhillin himself. I'm copying it here again now, longhand, I love it so much:

斷章[1]
你站在橋上看風景，看風景的人在樓上看你。
明月裝飾了你的窗子，你裝飾了別人的夢。

But when I turned to read one, he was frowning. I panicked, asking if there were anything wrong. I was clutching the book to my chest. I thought that maybe he'd take it away from me, the only gift he'd ever given to me. But then he said: *I forgot how annoying your voice is, to be honest.* Outside, someone was singing. It's an old folk song, one I don't really know. He was so calm, so careless. I picked up the bowl of soup and threw it toward his head. He ducked. Noodles and shards of porcelain streamed from behind. *What the hell?* He screamed. But I walked outside. I didn't have anything else to say.

Here's another poem that I like, by He Qifang[2]

He reaches out and pushes the door open. Alarmed at this lack of politeness? This is the outermost door, left unlocked during the day and only closed at night—and the peddler, who is not a rare guest in that house, knows all that perfectly well. Look at his calm, unhurried demeanor as he steps, the yellow wooden crate in his arms, through the door and into the main courtyard, paved with stones. Watch him as he walks forty or so paces across the courtyard and stops silently in front of the imposing double-doors with their rusted iron rings; the drum in his hand hoots once again...

I don't know how to write my own anymore. It's pathetic, you know? I'm sitting here writing this down, trying to convince myself that I feel fine about everything. But tomorrow I'll be waiting for him to call me, like I always do. My mom hasn't come home yet. I go and unlock the door for her, just in case she hasn't remembered her key.

The night bled into itself; overlapping shades of black. I clasped his hand like a child would. For years, I'd been at war with myself. I felt a sudden urge to tell him that I knew him, that even if he wouldn't introduce himself, I knew who he was. That I would recognize him no matter how many years had passed. That he'd haunted me all this while, now that it was happening, it felt almost peaceful.

We walked for what felt like hours. He hadn't spoken once since we'd left, and I felt so sad, so much wanting to know the same intimacy we'd known before. Had I offered him intimacy? Had I loved him well? Of course, the answer was no. I'd hated myself for so long now. Even in this moment, all that I could think of was myself. A selfish, miserable person who cared more about having my guilt absolved than reckoning with the pain I'd tortured him with.

Twigs crunched underneath my feet. I realized that it had been so long that surely the sun would be up by now, but no light had reached the earth.

Did he now control the universe?

The smell of red pine, its damp needles, the sticky scent of sap. I felt his body depart from mine and felt an unbearable emptiness, so heavy somehow, carve itself into my stomach.

"Come back," I whispered, stumbling forward. My hands found his chest and I sunk into him.

"How you changed over the years," Shenghang said. He stroked my hair as I sobbed. "What happened to the man I knew?"

"Shenghang," I said. "What happened to your poems?"

"I didn't realize you cared about them." I can hear his smile without seeing it, but it seemed sad. As if he had never gotten over it. He was always so touched by everything, everything. Once, he'd told me about a rabbit in the yard outside of his house. Its leg was broken, and it dragged itself along the grass, its ears flickering at the slightest sound. He'd tried to take it to the vet, but when he'd come back outside after getting his keys, the rabbit was gone.

Where did it go? He'd kept asking. *Where did it go?*

It's probably gone, I said. *Don't worry about it. It's fine.*

You used to love rabbits, he'd said, and stopped speaking after that.

I'd never been able to not hurt him.

"I did care. I loved your writing."

He didn't respond.

"I loved your poems. I loved watching you read them."

"You said you hated my voice that day. You made me feel so terrible."

"I didn't mean it."

As he rises, the cold moon rises with him, arcing now above the trees.

"What about when you killed me?" He's begging now

for an answer, no longer composed. "Did you mean it when you murdered me?"

Then the moon splits in half. The fragments shudder for a moment before finally allowing the sun to rise.

Tu-er Shen, 1994

I will tell it all from the end and then back to the beginning.

He knew I often kept the door unlocked for my mom. He'd been hanging out with those guys from school more. Xiao Feng and his friends. I was lying in bed. The door opened downstairs and I thought my mom had come home. But it wasn't just one set of feet, it was more. Xiao Feng had a baseball bat. They took turns. *You go ahead*, Xiao Feng said. I could tell he was drunk. He stumbled toward him, holding the bat out. *If he's not your little boyfriend, then you do it too.* But he just stood there. Xiao Feng shrugged and picked it up again, holding it high above his head. Over and over, I cried out for him. It would have been better, honestly, if he'd just joined in with the rest of them. But that cowardice is what killed me. I knew what he'd probably told them. You can always blame someone else for the way that you are.

I will tell it all from the end and then back to the beginning.

He came back for me later on, right before my mother came home. I can still hear her screams. I remember that he held me as I was dying. *I'm sorry, I'm sorry*, he kept saying. He never did tell me that he loved me. Unlike me, he didn't get a second chance. Despite myself, I find myself thinking from time to time that perhaps it would've been nice to live out the centuries with him. Why choose me? This is the question I ask the most often. I'm in the business of forgiving and blessing those who come by my temple. But I'm also in the business of revenge.

The temple grounds have been swept recently. Offerings decorate the altar upon which the rabbit god sits with his red mask, furs gathered over his shoulders. The god taps the statue, amused. "Does he look like me?" he says. No one else is beside him in the early morning fog. His face falls. Suddenly, he wraps his arms around an empty space, as if trying to love the air that a boy once inhabited.

The flashlight is found, still emitting a weak light, the next day. His supervisor figures that he's quit the job like so many others have. But then a day spills into a week. His father screams at the authorities to investigate. His mother is a piece of furniture; never moving from one spot. His uniform is never found. A year later, a book arrives at their house. There's no return address on the package, and no title on its cover when the father opens it. The father flips open to the first page. Disgust grows on his face, rage, but he must keep reading. He must know the truth. But page after page, he realizes, is the same unfinished poem, over and over again:

Whistle cleaving voice
Body punctuating body

Boy and ghost, together

He throws it into the trash.

If you ever go to the temple, decide for yourself. Does he look like the mysterious boy you read about in this story? Could such a weak man truly be venerated as a god? Do not be anything but honest. If you decide your answer is "Yes," say a prayer. Ask for wealth, for Tu'Er Shen to fix your relationship. Tell him of your sins or your love for someone who does not love you back. Light the incense and leave.

Sometimes, though no one sees it, the rabbit's eye looks as if it's leaking.

Shenghang never did finish the last line of the poem. Who's really to blame?

GOOD ROUTE, BAD ROUTE

We've been developing this game for about 3 years now —*Mistaken Person: Love is Destiny*. The publisher I work for is called wataame. It's a big one. You've probably heard of it, if you're into this sort of thing. Some of our most popular games are *Okonomiyaki, Honey + Vengeance, Literature Love Club,* and *dokidoki donburi!.*

Mistaken Person: Love is Destiny is expected to be one of our biggest games yet. The latest installment in the *dokidoki donburi* series.

In the last game of the series, *dokidoki donburi: Tokyo terror!!,* you play a normal guy working the line at a chain restaurant who's in love with the waitress, Ami. But, of course, something bad happens and suddenly you and your coworkers are trying to defeat a yakuza boss, the owner of the restaurant. Surprise! Turns out the boss is Ami's dad. That game was a big success.

The one before that was poorly animated, had bad story writing, and all the girls had the same personality, more or less. Not even worth talking about. *Tokyo terror!!*

was the one that propelled us into the spotlight. And *Mistaken Person: Love is Destiny* is going to be even better than that because people want the real stuff now—they don't want to be in the mafia or whatever. They want to see themselves and the world as is: bleak and scary and caustic —but they also want to see themselves triumph over it. Even if it's only in a game.

Wei is my only friend here. Or at least Wei is the only person I can tolerate. The rest of the guys I work with are fine, easy enough to chat with as we refill our tea at the hot drink bar during lunch, talking about the government and the weather. Or talking about the stuff we're watching or listening to as we grab dishes of egg omelet and bean sprouts, potato salad and miso soup, and put them on our trays. But that's all I can talk about with them. Every time I try to say something else, talk about my life or what I do outside of here, I freeze up and that's that. We make polite excuses and go sit at our respective tables.

Wei is different because he has a lot to say and because on some level, we get each other. Or at least I think we do. Sometimes I worry he's just my friend because we grew up together, but he's the type of guy who would stop talking to you if he disliked you so I don't really believe it's that.

"I wanna get really drunk tonight," Wei says as we sit down to eat. "Like super fucking wasted." He always gets the same thing every lunch: rice and whatever vegetable option they have, plus five packets of natto (*for the probiotics, you know?*)

"Right. For sure."

"You should come out too," he says, slapping my shoulder. "I only ever get to see you once or twice a month outside of work these days. Let's get out and meet some babes. You haven't dated anyone in forever."

I shrug my shoulders up and then down.

"Why don't you try a dating app? Or actually, wait. I know someone. Real cute, works at the flower shop down the street. I went to elementary school with her. Want me to introduce you guys?"

"I'm okay."

Wei looks at me for a half a beat then rips open the small packets of mustard and sauce, mixes them into the natto until they're sticky and white. He does this three more times before dumping it all onto his bowl of rice.

"Why don't you ever get natto?" he asks. "It's good for you."

"I don't like the smell."

"Get over it."

"I'll try."

Wei is the lead programmer at wataame. When we were kids we built gundams, made our stag beetles fight, all of that. But we had the most fun when we were playing video games: *King's Field, Panzer Dragoon, Star Ocean, Tactics Ogre*, eating chips and drinking energy drinks until they made us sick. His family is Chinese, they owned a store that sold used electronics, which was how our families became friends. I was the half-Chinese kid whose mom couldn't speak any elementary-level Japanese. I was lonely in a way my child mind understood but didn't know how to help. And fate or God or whatever you believe in made me a nerd who loved games and needed a used Nintendo 64 (because we couldn't afford a new one) and brought us to Wei's tiny shop.

"What are you doing later tonight?" Wei asks as we pick up our trays and move them into the dish bin.

Lunch is over and everyone's going back to work or if they've done enough, they're going home. People push past each other to get to the elevators, thinking about love or work or sex or pissing, whatever.

"I don't know. I have to do some more work at home, I think."

"Alright," Wei says, throwing on his jacket. "If you wanna come hang out, let me know. I could show you the gundam I'm working on now."

"Okay. I will."

"Later."

He shakes a cigarette from his jacket pocket and puts on his sunglasses, walking out into the parking lot. I watch him light the cigarette as he leans against the car door, smiling at something on his phone. Then for some reason he looks up at the sun very fast, his head turning to look at it. As if confused that such a thing exists, or that it is so warm. Then he gets into his car and drives away.

When I get home to my apartment I feel like my head is about to explode so I grab a beer from the fridge. There's some leftover karaage from the supermarket so I heat it up in the microwave and even though it's not warm enough I decide it'll do. I sit down on the couch and contemplate jacking off and decide it's not worth the effort. I have work to do.

I'm the only one that can do this. I haven't told anyone about it, but I think it's a better way to test *Mistaken*

Person: Love is Destiny out anyway. Nobody needs to know about it. I designed the damn game, after all.

I put on the suit that the MC wears—jeans and a white t-shirt. And my headset looks like the baseball cap the MC wears, just with a couple of knobs on it that allows me to rearrange my body into a collection of pixels; transfer what we may term a "soul" into the body of the character; and when I'm done or if things go really bad (say, if I encounter a glitch that may cause my body physical harm), I can catapult myself out of the game. It's only happened once.

I don the headset and the white t-shirt and the jeans. I switch the knob to ON and feel little pieces of myself begin to get fuzzy as I start to transfer over. First the legs, then the arms, then all the rest. I don't know what my physical shell looks like while I'm out. I guess it could, potentially, be dangerous—a robber could break in while I'm still in the game, but it hasn't happened yet. And I'm too lazy to try and do anything about it now anyway.

I fade. Or rather I transfer existence and suddenly I'm inside of this world, blinking and looking around where I'm at now.

There's a lot of noise and the smell of meat cooking so even before everything starts appearing I know I'm at the Korean BBQ place. This is one of the three places I'm able to go with Risa—KBBQ, the club, and the arcade.

I've completed almost all of Risa's Routes:

Good Route: She becomes a successful DJ and you're a supportive husband.

Bad Route: (I'll tell you what happens there in a minute.)

The only one left is the Neutral Route:

"So here we are again," Risa says. The pork belly crackles over the grill. She flips it over with a pair of tongs, grabs some pieces of kalbi, slaps them on. Everything is dark and smoky. Beer mugs clink and people lean over their tables, yell over the noise of everyone else. Servers run about looking frazzled.

While our kalbi grills, Risa takes out a pack of cigarettes and lights one. She takes a drag, plays with her eyebrow piercing. It's one of her main character traits—cigarettes, self-masochism, being loud. She's abrasive and hard to win over, so it's especially rewarding when she opens up to you.

"So here we are," I reply. A man bumps into my chair and sloshes some sesame oil onto the table. Then onto me.

"Ah, sorry," he says.

"Don't worry about it," I say. Risa grabs a napkin and throws it my way, and I dab some of the sauce off my pants. I consider asking her for one of the cigarettes before she snatches them away.

"I've only got two left," she says. "So what was it that you wanted to ask me?"

Here's one of the crucial points of the game.

Selection A: *So what really happened to your parents?*

This leads you to the Bad Route/Ending. Risa tells you what happened to her parents, you try to get Risa to go to rehab, she does, and the doctor ends up being someone else from her past who messed her up. It's so traumatizing that Risa loses her mind.

If you want the Good Ending, ask her to do something fun.

Selection B: *Do you wanna go to the arcade?*

"Do you wanna go to the arcade?" I ask.

"Sure," she says. She crushes her cigarette in the ashtray, sloughs down the rest of her beer, shoves a bunch of beef in her mouth. "I wanna play Beatmania."

We leave the restaurant. It's dark outside and Risa lights another cigarette, looks up at the sky.

"Do you hang out with a lot of people outside of here?" she asks.

This is one of the components of this thing I've made. Risa isn't just choosing from preset dialogue options right now. In choosing to input my own data, my own soul makeup into this game, I think it bled into the other characters.

Which has been good and bad.

"I mostly just hang out with Wei."

Risa always wears dark eyeliner, way too heavy. Often dons shirts with metal or noise bands on them. Oftentimes, she looks pissed or annoyed. But sometimes she just looks like most of us: scared, confused, human.

Risa blows her bangs out of her eyes and they flutter right back down. She tries again and finally gives up. "I get tired of hanging out with Megumi and Bee all the time. They're so annoying."

Megumi is the quintessential cute girl of *Mistaken Person: Love is Destiny*. She likes shopping, sweets, and appears ultra-happy all the time until it's revealed how deeply insecure she is. She developed a severe eating disorder and got plastic surgery for how bullied she was in school. Didn't leave her house for months and months and still struggles with it sometimes. She wants to be a model, but she's so scared of rejection she'd rather not even bother.

Megumi's Routes are:

Good: You help her accept that rejection is a part of human experience. She gets scouted by a modeling agency and walks for all the major designers. She's busy but you two take date nights to get dessert. Your favorite is creme brûlée, hers is strawberry crepes.

Neutral: She ends up getting gigs doing commercials. Yogurt, cell phones, tooth paste. She doesn't mind it and sometimes you walk through Shibuya and see her brushing her teeth and smiling on the huge screen as hundreds of people walk around you, looking at their phones or talking to their partners.

Bad: You are ignorant to her hints that she's not really the person she pretends to be. She ends up dating some guy who's a model and won't ever ask her questions about her life because he doesn't care. She's miserable and gets sicker but she pretends she's fine.

There's a sound like *bang* and me and Risa look over. Someone's ran into a curb at the KBBQ. We make eye contact with the man inside his car and he sheepishly grins, like *sorry*. Then he drives away.

"Anyways," Risa says, "Megumi is starting to get on my nerves." Risa can pretend she doesn't like Megumi; her big fake lashes or designer bags or frilly dresses, but she has a soft spot for her. Like she does for everyone.

Risa and I get to the arcade and it's loud and the lights are bright and I'm feeling overwhelmed. Maybe I don't want to try to complete a Route right now but Risa's already got her tokens for Beatmania, she's inserted them into the slot. She's immersed in mixing and scratching the vinyl controllers, mashing the buttons with ease. All the other characters around us are blurred, just NPCs mumbling and playing their own games. Everywhere pop music blares and anime girls' voices tell you that you're doing a good job.

Risa gets PERFECT and lifts up her arms in triumph.

"I did it!" she says. "I did it!"

I clap like I do every time. She gets PERFECT every time. It's impressive.

"So what are you going to do about Bee?" she asks.

The dialogue buttons are now floating above her head.

A: *Nothing, I'm in love with you.*

B: *Why do you ask?*

I choose B this time.

"Because I think you should talk to her. She seems like she's going through a hard time."

A: *I'll do it some other time.*

B: *You're right. I think I should do that.*

I choose B.

Risa smiles. "Good job," she says. "You're a good friend, you know? I hope we can continue hanging out after this. I applied for a couple of jobs, by the way. Will you come visit me if I get the one at the record store?"

"Of course."

We fast forward from the arcade to Risa's Neutral Ending. You visit her at the record store, buy a Soichi Terada vinyl you've been wanting.

"Go talk to Bee," she says as she flips through a box of cassettes that someone brought in. "Or else you're a pussy."

"Alright, alright, I'll go."

"Love you man," she says. And she does. And I'm scared of her love and everyone else's, even Wei's, scared of my parents' love and my love for people.

Most of all, though, I'm scared of Bee's love. Or more importantly, the lack of it.

The last shot I see of Risa is of her laughing, pretending to punch the camera as bewildered customers look on.

I twist one knob on the side of my hat. The arcade scene

fades, becomes blurred, becomes pixels, then just before it becomes nothing, I quickly toggle the other knob.

There's always kind of a disconcerting feeling when you feel your soul being arranged, transferred back from one thing to another. As if it is something tangible, understandable. It's a swift *whoosh* like getting sucked into a vacuum cleaner ... then I am back in my living room on the couch.

My apartment looks so much more depressing after being in the game. I glance at the plastic remains of trash scattered on the coffee table, decide to ignore it. My computer screen glows in the dark, the only source of light.

My phone goes off. It's Wei calling.

"Yo."

I can hear him clicking around on his keyboard, the firing of bullets coming from his screen. "What's up, man?"

"Not much."

"That's always your answer—FUCK!" Wei says. Something erupts in the background.

I want to tell Wei what I'm feeling but I don't know how so I listen to him shoot down more spaceships, fight more monsters.

"Um. I. I actually—"

"Do you want to go to Akiba tomorrow? Animate is having a sale on a bunch of figures tomorrow."

"Ok. Ok, that sounds like something I could do."

"I've been wanting this Mayoi figure for a while. Super rare. You can actually open her backpack up, and it comes with different outfits as well. Great deal."

"I don't really need anything. But I don't mind coming along. Maybe they'll have some promotional stuff for the new Evangelion movie."

"Right, totally, for sure. Oh yeah, I meant to ask. How's Bee? Talk to her lately?"

And suddenly I feel myself shutting down. My body disintegrating into pixels, atoms, whatever.

I hear Wei take off his headset, it makes a small clatter. He pauses the game.

"Still like that, huh?" he says.

"Yeah."

"I've been meaning to ask you. Do you—" He hesitates. "Do you think it was a good idea to make this character just like her?"

"I don't think so. But I won't be the one playing it anyway."

"Okay. Well, I mean, if we pushed the release date back a little..."

"It's fine." Suddenly I feel like I am drowning. A sea of plasma. "I'll talk to you tomorrow, alright?"

"Just be careful," Wei says. Which means he knows, more or less.

"Ok."

"Later, man." Wei hangs up the phone.

Megumi and Risa weren't based off of anyone really. Just an assortment of characteristics from different people I had come in contact with in my life, different girls I had met. Things I liked or disliked about other people.

Bee is just one person. One person whose face can remain inside of *Mistaken Person: Love is Destiny*, even if her real face begins to slowly fade from my memory since we decided to not speak any more. Or I guess she decided to not speak to me. I haven't checked her social media or anything.

But she's still here, at least, if not in any other place in my life.

I reach into the fridge for a beer. I finish my beer and then another and then suddenly I've drank six. I say *fuck it* and pour myself vodka and then it's the whole bottle. I puke once. Then another beer.

I manage to stumble toward where I've thrown the cap on the couch, twist all the knobs from muscle memory. If I don't think about it, then I don't have to think about it.

The Good Ending for Bee is one I made up, of course: We're still together, and she's holding my hand as we walk through the garden, seeing the names of different trees and she looks up at me and her cheeks are pink from the cold and she's smiling.

The Neutral Ending is Bee and I are still friends and we don't bear any resentment and we've both found other people and sometimes we talk about the things we enjoy, new music from bands we liked, new books, funny clips of TV comedians we liked.

The Bad Ending and the true ending are the same, of course.

A: *Bee, you are the only girl I've ever loved and there will never be anyone I'll love again.*

B: *I am sorry for what I have done and will do in the future and everything in between.*

It won't matter either way.

I ask myself why I'm doing this. We have actual game testers on the team. Why repeat a bad thing a second time? Am I trying to punish myself for not being a better boyfriend, a better me—someone better in holding together both myself and the person she became as she started unraveling?

The soul drifts. The world begins to form around me. I'm in the garden. The small lake in the middle is frozen over. I wonder if the fish are still alive. I look up at the trees and their bare limbs look back at me.

Bee's sitting on a bench and she has two cups of coffee beside her. Her face is in her hands, her hair covering her like moss. I wobble toward her with a big smile on my face.

She looks up at me and there's tears collecting on her eyelashes, forming small clumps. She's wearing the hat we bought together at the boutique she likes so much, a red knit beanie. I'm remembering even through the drunken haze. I can prove it to her this time that I'm still me even when I'm like this.

"You're fucking drunk again," she says.

I try to take a seat beside her and one of the coffees spills into the grass.

"Oops! Guess I'll just have to buy you another. You like those honey lattes the most, right? We can go to that one cafe after this!"

I put my arm around her, place my head on her shoulder. Her body doesn't react. I'm looking up at her face. She won't even look at me. There are no tears anymore. Just something blank and unknowable.

"Oh," I say, jumping up. I fall over and pick myself up and Bee still isn't looking at me. "We can even go to that cake shop you like too! And maybe after that we can watch a movie, finish that one horror movie about the mom who gets possessed by a demon we started the other—"

"I'm leaving you."

And I feel my heart stop. I don't feel so drunk anymore. Of course I remember every single part of this.

"What do you mean?"

She shakes a pack of cigarettes out of her bag, lights one. Blows the smoke out. Did I ever tell you that she had the most beautiful eyebrows in the world? What a weird thing. But it's true. Beautiful eyebrows and a beautiful mole near her mouth and a beautiful little nose—beautiful Bee.

"I don't want to be with you anymore."

I sit in the middle of the pathway. There's no one else in the garden. It starts snowing and the beauty of it makes me feel angry. Sitting isn't good enough so I lay down. I can feel myself shaking.

"Who is it?"

"There's nobody. But I know it's not you."

I'm crying now and staring at her shoes because it's too hard to look at her face. I hear her start crying again too. A noise like *ah, ah, ah, ah, ah, ah, ah,* is coming from somewhere and I realize it's me.

"Please. Please. Pleasepleasepleaseplease—"

"My sister. She killed herself yesterday. I tried to call you but you wouldn't answer. Probably passed out somewhere drunk, right? Probably tried to reach for your phone and couldn't get to it in time. Or maybe you just didn't give a shit. That's probably right. You didn't give a shit."

And that's it and now Bee is the one spilling the coffee and she's throwing things, anything she can find in her bag, spinning out of control, she's running out of the garden toward the sidewalk and I try to catch up to her as the snow starts falling heavy.

Then something weird happens. Something that's not supposed to happen. Bee is suddenly not this memory. She stops in the middle of the sidewalk and when I reach her, she looks at me with something like love.

And she twists the knobs on the hat. No other character in this game can see those. When I'm in here it just looks like a hat. How?

I start to fade away and I want to see her for one last time but she's waving at me, goodbye goodbye. This isn't how it ended. What happened was much worse. Right before I blink out, shift back into the real world, I see her mouthing something but I can't make out what she's saying. She's saying it over and over again but I can't hear her and then I'm back on my couch and I'm sobbing. Everything is quiet now. Seems like there's not even traffic. The night shifts into morning. A bird flits past my window and the tears won't come any more but I can feel my eyes burning.

The Bad Ending, the one you'll encounter when you're playing the game, concludes with you two screaming at each other and she's spitting at you and you're trying to tell her you did love her, loved her sister too, loved her family, and she says, "She didn't deserve to die. But maybe you do."

And that's not actually what Bee said when it happened. She said something like, "Just stay away from me forever. Get some help." And she gave me 100,000 yen. But the *Mistaken Person: Love is Destiny* version makes for better dialogue, one that will really pull at the player's heartstrings.

What's so bad about the thing that just happened is that even in the game, Bee was the one saving me. Like she always did.

––––

As I sobered up the next day, I focused on remembering the

motions of Bee's mouth until I figured out what she was saying. I wrote it down so I wouldn't forget:

"I forgive you."

That's what she said.

After *Mistaken Person: Love is Destiny,* I decided to not make romance games any more. I left wataame and switched to a different company, made RPGs with cool weaponry and villains. Still stayed in touch with Wei. Even went to drink with Wei once, like he wanted me too. I got one hi-ball and left.

The game did well. Made a lot of money, actually. But a lot of reviewers said they were confused with the MC's interactions with Bee, that her storyline didn't seem as smooth as the others—how did the MC start drinking? When? And there's a glitch at the end of one of Risa's Routes that we had to patch up because it kept freezing. Stuff like that.

I am tired of seeing the human heart so easily and carelessly displayed.

I didn't touch *Mistaken Person: Love is Destiny* after its release. I smashed the hat, destroyed all the knobs. I want to tell you I stopped drinking so much at home but that isn't true.

I think about contacting Bee though. I open LINE, close it. I still remember her username. Maybe she's unblocked me. Or maybe I can even e-mail her: Was that you? Was it really you there with me?

But I never contact her. Maybe one day she'll talk to me again—ask me the name of that author I recommended to her, the name of that trail that we hiked once in autumn.

Or we'll run into each other by accident and she'll be happier now and still as funny as she was when I first knew her, telling me ridiculous stories, flapping her hands around.

Besides, it's not like I don't know the answers to those questions. Of course I do. Of course.

HOME VIDEO

The town we live in is nameless. Even if you tried to find it on the map, you wouldn't be able to.

I think I must've had parents at some point. But nobody seems to know whose theirs are, or how they even got here in the first place. Nobody could tell you anything about this town's history, not even the really old folks like Ms. L. or Mr. A. Sometimes people will come nosing around to try and find out if maybe we're all just pulling a big trick on them, if we're actually just hiding something. One of them kept asking and asking what my name was even though I told him I didn't have one. He told Minnow that he wanted to ask me about some of my powers and then pulled me away before she got a chance to say no.

"Little girl, are you okay? Is there something bad happening to you and all the other kids in this place?"

Above him, the dark crimson sun crested and made a perfect arc above the river.

"Mister, turn around and look at how pretty that sun is."

But he didn't turn around.

"What do you all do here? How long has this place been around?"

"I don't know what to tell you, Mister. None of us know, and that's just the truth."

His mouth got small and scrunched. He wrote some things down and told Minnow thanks for letting him talk to me, she's a very special young girl. Minnow didn't say anything but puffed away at her cigarette. Later on, she would tell me I did a good job.

Later that week, a bunch of men came wearing important looking hats and seemed very confident that they would be able to do something. Emphasis on "something," because I don't even know if they knew how to go about anything. It only took about an hour or so for them to get dreamy looks on their faces, talking about how beautiful this little town was, how bright and colorful it was. They drove away smiling, but kind of confused, as if they knew they'd forgotten something important but didn't know what it was.

However much they wanted to help us, it didn't matter. They were just as stupid and unremarkable as we were, and I didn't want to be saved anyway. Peter would be the one to save me, like he always promised.

Emil and Turnip had been taken away somewhere. I don't think they were dead, but then again, you never had a way of knowing. If people stopped being able to perform, if they lost some of their abilities over time, they'd have to go in to get "repairs." Terra hadn't been able to make anything grow in ages, and she was taken off of shows. All she did now was lay in bed, staring up at the ceiling. Right before she'd went missing and came back again, she'd grown me and Minnow and Peter a cherry tree in the backyard.

I went to visit her yesterday while Idaho was gone. Terra didn't look at me when I walked in, but I thought that maybe deep down, she was happy to see me. I sat on the little wooden chair next to her bed and started pleating her hair. When she was still doing okay, she'd always kept it in braids. But now, Idaho never tried to braid it, and it was always a tangled mess.

"Peter said we're leaving tomorrow. He's figured a lot of stuff out, apparently. I'm sorry I won't be able to take you with us, but I'm going to try and come back for you. He told me there might be a way to do that."

I finished one braid and pulled her head up to get the other half. Her hair was yellow and brittle like straw underneath my fingers.

"I'm going to miss you a lot. I miss you a lot already, because you can't talk to me anymore and we can't go outside together. And now Emil and Turnip are gone too. I gotta tell you, Terra. I'm a little scared. But Peter pinky-promised. Do you think that means we'll be alright?"

I finished braiding her hair and laid her head back down. She blinked a couple of times, but that was all. Maybe she had been forcing herself to try and cry.

"Bye, Terra."

I opened the door and walked outside, making sure to close the door tight behind me. In another world, I'd be the one who couldn't move and stayed in bed all the time, and Terra would be the one leaving me. That's how I'd have preferred for it to go. But at the same time, it hurt to think about, because I know what I'd be feeling in that moment: betrayed.

To take my mind off of things the next day, I ended up watching a lot of educational shows about the ocean on TV. Everything was all fuzzy-looking, but I tried to imagine what TV would look like in the other place me and Peter would be going. Maybe it would be really HD, or "High-definition." Peter said that there's stuff in the world that can look like that.

The show was about an octopus. It was pink and very beautiful, its legs like ribbons in the water. When I asked Minnow once about why the testing center was so far away, and if Peter would ever be able to leave, she didn't say anything. She just said that these things take time, but I don't know what she meant by "things," or how much time was too much, so I didn't bring it up again.

I walked to the refrigerator and drank some milk, making sure not to get any on the quilts and blankets. The man on TV explained that people might not think of octopi as smart, given that 1) they're animals 2) they have weird-shaped heads, but in fact, they're super smart.

"Observe," he said, "Pinky escaping from his tank." I observed Mr. Pinky, a red-and-blue octopus, shimmying his way up to the top of his small cylinder-shaped tank. He moved like he was dancing, his arms bouqueting in the water. As soon as he got to the top, he started unscrewing it with his infinite arms till it popped open. He was really remarkable, Mr. Pinky. The cameras followed him as he pushed off, gliding his way toward freedom. And then he was gone.

"Imagine you're 600 pounds," the TV announcer said. "You don't have any bones, which means you're able to go just about anywhere. You can even squeeze through a space as small as a quarter!"

I shut my eyes and listened to the fan whirl above my head, the cicadas chirp-chirp-chirping away out in the yard. Just like how Pinky made his escape, I could see myself unscrewing the top of the shack they kept Peter in, carrying Peter away, circling high above this entire town. I didn't have any bones, which means we couldn't get hurt no matter if I started falling from somewhere up high or not. I was maybe even a little bit poisonous too.

"Whether Pinky made it to the ocean is something we don't know, but one thing's for certain: he's one remarkable creature." They played some music and then moved on to a commercial about carpet cleaner, at which point I got out my notebook and started to write a little story about what happened to him afterward to show to Peter.

Mr. Pinky is living a really grate life in the see. He made a lot of new frends and they threw him a birday party with a see weed cake. And he was reenouned for being a master escaper. The maior gave him a metal for it, and he took all of his frends to the grate beyond. Go Mr. Pinky.

The fan sputtered and turned off.

"Goddamnit," Minnow said. She slapped it a couple of times, and it came back on for a few minutes before stopping again. "Guess I'll have to go get another one from the junkyard."

The junkyard was where most of us got our stuff. Donors would send things there: if they were really impressed, they'd send a bunch of good stuff. If the shows had just been alright, they'd send stuff like broken fans or old, dusty rugs. I'd guess that we could probably get a really nice fan if she went now, because apparently, they'd all thought Emil and Turnip had been marvelous: the burning boy and the one who could cannibalize himself, only to have his hands and feet grow back afterward, made a spectacular duo. They didn't know that Turnip had lost it, began eating bits of Emil too while in his fugue state: by the time the show had ended and everyone rushed in to pull him out, all that was left of him was half of a face. His eye was the only thing that could move, and it flitted around, panicked, as Turnip screamed and screamed. I had been there watching them. Turnip's tears froze on his face like white slugs as he thrashed around; the grass around us grew stiff with snow. No one had suspected that Turnip had been sick and that his body wouldn't obey him no more.

I know it's wrong to think like this, but maybe there hadn't been anything wrong with Turnip. Maybe it was just everyone else's fault, and he'd had enough.

Minnow started putting on her boots to head out to the junkyard. My stomach hurt from eating so much ice cream.

"Minnow."

"What is it?" she was halfway out the door, a cigarette already lit in her mouth.

"If I died or got lost, would you be sad?"

She looked at me for a minute before shaking her head.

"You really are a stupid girl, aren't you?" she said, and slammed the door.

I gathered the cherries from outside the yard to take to Peter. It was spring, and they'd turned nice and shiny, like little Christmas ornaments. I'd also seen those on TV, too. Christmas was a holiday some people celebrated in December, and they'd hang up little orbs on a tree and sing around it. I thought that was really weird and a little stupid. If their god had died on a tree, shouldn't they hate trees? Instead, here they were, singing around it. If I were that god, I'd have told the tree to fall over and kill them.

The smell of fried fish wafted toward me. I looked around and saw Mr. A staring at these fish swimming in the pond outside his house. Apparently, he'd used to be able to transform into one. Oarfish or starfish or orcas, you name it. But one day he woke up and he couldn't do it anymore. All he could do now was stare at them, wishing he could return to being the way he was back in his days of youth.

"How're you doing, sweetheart?" he asked. Above us, a small bird flew by, carrying a twig in its beak. We watched as it hopped on top of the cherry tree, adding the twig to its nest. I could see the raw pink necks of babies sticking out their mouths for lunch, but it seemed momma didn't have anything for them. She flew away again, leaving them to cry.

"I'm okay." I raised my basket of cherries for him to see. "I'm going to go see Peter."

Mr. A clucked his tongue. "They've had that boy in there for too long," he muttered. "Too young to be putting his body through all of that."

"Minnow said I don't know about what's bad or good for him because I'm too young."

"Minnow, she don't know what she's talking about. And people wouldn't think she's as dumb as she is if she would just shut up sometimes."

"Isn't that sort of mean?"

"Yes, honey. But Mr. A is feeling a little mean today."

He walked over to me and pulled something out of his overall pocket. They were two small marbles, with pretty flower designs on them.

"You give these to Peter. I know how he likes his math experiments."

"Thank you, Mr. A."

He waved. The fish glistened in the sun, and I felt a deep hollow feeling inside of me as I walked the road to where Peter was. The forest grew thicker. I walked past Ms. L's house with its hundreds of tin cans and metallic pinwheels and headed fast into the forest. I remembered levitating inside of her messy living room, Terra in the background sleeping, curled up in snake-form. *No one understands you but that's okay*, she would say as I practiced levitating in the middle of her messy living room, one of her rock hard cinnamon scones in my hand. *Ms. L always understands.*

Me and Peter used to pretend we were Ms. L's kids, but after a while, it had gotten depressing. She had been disappearing for a while now, whole parts of her going invisible without her wanting them to. The donors used to love her, loved how she could flicker in and out of being at will. But she had gotten old, and ratings went down. Eventually, I had taken her place. When I forced myself to go visit her now, she couldn't even speak. I would knock on the door, and it would open, a cup of tea and a plate of scones hovering before me. As I sat down on the couch, a piece of paper would appear on the table. "Talk to me," Ms. L would say. "I'm so lonely." So I talked for hours about dragonflies, about orchards and little beads of dew atop leaves, and fans that worked poorly, and television shows about people far away from us. After I was too tired to speak any more, we sat there without doing anything until I decided I was ready to go. She didn't ever ask for me to stay longer. I think she must have felt embarrassed.

The wind scraped against my cheeks, and I pulled my

scarf up around my face. There was a small hole Terra and I would throw rocks into, watching them tumble down into the nothingness. We figured that one day, we would have thrown enough rocks to fill it. I think we were close to getting there, but then one day Terra got too tired to come play rocks with me. And now she laid in bed all day, staring at the ceiling, from which vines and branches would grow until someone came to prune them.

I was getting close to where Peter was now. Ahead of me, a thin light emanated through the darkness. A boy with overgrown wings, one crooked and slouched on the side, sat atop the roof. He started smiling as I approached. For a moment, I felt like everything was still the same as it had been the first day we met: the grass, overgrown and wet with last night's rain; the horse out in its stable braying in a way that seemed tortured and yearning. For what, I don't know: maybe buckets of pale green apples, a chance to do life over again, to roam the plains of Honduras, untethered and free.

"Peter," I said. "I've brought you some more cherries, and some marbles, too."

But he seemed so excited that he didn't even parse together what I said. In front of him was a huge piece of paper with scribbled equations and diagrams on it. He spit and wiped his mouth with a dirt-covered hand.

"I think I've gotten it," he said. "I think I finally figured out how it all works."

You're the only one that doesn't lie, Peter had said when I had told him I would always take care of him. That one day, his wings would work again, and we could get away from here. But I still couldn't figure out what a lie was. Everything, eventually, could be broken apart. People didn't mind whether what they were watching was real or fake, or stop to consider if it was immoral: Peter was the boy who couldn't die, no matter how many times you shot him or split his head open with an axe. Eventually, he'd just come back to life again. And the first thing he'd say when he woke up was always the same: "Did I finally get to die this time?"

Now, Peter was looking at me, holding out a hand for me to grasp onto. I placed mine gently in his and floated up next to him.

He pointed at its center. "You ever wondered how we all ended up here? Or how none of us have memories?"

I thought about it for a little bit. "Yes."

"And what did you come up with?"

"Nothing."

"Do you like anything about this town?"

"I like you. And I like the sun."

"How do you think all those people find us?"

"I don't know."

"Those guys, they're all donors. They put money into us, place bets. I don't know if any of them ever figure out this is a testing center or not, but sooner or later, they start feeling bad about themselves. And so they try to come and rescue us, but only because they feel bad. Not because they actually care."

I reached into my pocket to pull out my story about Mr. Pinky. "I wrote you this story about an octopus. I learned about him on TV."

"Thank you, sweetie. But we don't have time to think about that right now."

"I didn't have time to try and do that thing you asked me to do."

"That's alright. Just show me what you've been practicing for all this time."

"Okay."

I let go of Peter's hand. He squinted up at me as I floated past the trees and the birds and into the sky, into the atmosphere, floating as high as I could go. I angled myself toward the direction that Peter told me to go, this place right in the middle that he'd made me memorize from all different positions from where we were on the ground. I reached my fingers up to touch a cloud. Just like he'd said, these ones didn't dissolve or move at all. The only thing I could feel was something solid and thick, like glass.

I came back down to where Peter was waiting for me.

"Did you feel it?" he asked. I could tell he was losing energy. None of his wounds had ever closed up, and at this point, his entire body was one gigantic scar. Raised, pink scratches up and down every surface of his body. A red ring glistened around his neck, where they had sawed him open last week.

"Yes."

"Do you want to see Emil and Turnip again?"

"Yes."

"The reason why Terra didn't make it out was that she went the wrong way. She'd almost gotten it right, but she didn't go up. She went down."

I thought about the big old hole, and us throwing rocks into it to see if it would fill up. Sometimes, we'd think we'd hear something, and we'd run away shrieking but secretly excited.

"What's down there?"

"Our memories. Names. People we used to be before coming here. I think that's what made her so crazy: She saw too much. Down's exactly where they want you to go. It's a trick."

Peter raised his arms toward me. His wings lifted a little

in the breeze. He'd explained to me what would happen as we got closer to the sun. We would melt, but we wouldn't die. We'd just join together, and once we were out, we'd be free.

I scooped his frail body up into my arms. He smiled at me with his brown teeth and I thought about how he looked as beautiful as the sea. I pushed off with one foot, and then the other, and we hovered above the roof for a moment. I guess both of us wanted a chance to say goodbye to this place one last time. And then I shot us up into the sky, going as fast as I could. Tears streamed out of Peter's face and I could tell how cold he was, but I could see the cloud above us, the one that wasn't like the others. Peter stretched out his hand and waved. And then the sky shattered.

Glass pierced our skin. I watched the drops of blood floating past us as we flew. I could see people above us now, people waving and dancing before us, and I knew that we were close. I took one last look at Peter. His eyes were black now, no light inside of them, but they made me feel the same as always: happy and safe. But that was only for a moment.

The figures were clearer now, and the world below us was shutting itself away, the glass forming over the town like a giant scab. Fog was everywhere, and I gripped Peter tighter, my arms shaking.

"What are these things?" I asked, but Peter didn't reply. His eyes were closed and I could see his mouth moving, trying to say something, but I couldn't make it out.

All around us were white crawling things. Things that looked like humans but were bleached white, crawling on all fours in the fog. They were naked, and when one of them turned toward me, I saw a familiar face. Emil's round, childish face, but his eyes were stabbed out. Black blood leaked from them as he crawled toward me, one arm outstretched as if in welcome.

Peter dropped from my arms. I thought about Mr. Pinky and his fantastic escape, how he had managed to unscrew the entire world, as he shook violently, his wings falling off of him. The fog passed across his body and sucked away his skin. Slowly, the color left his face, and as I felt myself folding over, I thought I saw a large finger twisting its way into his eye. If he screamed or not, I didn't know; all I could hear was a horrible, guttural silence.

The claw, once it had finished picking out both of Peter's eyes, changed directions. It crawled toward me like a spider, and perched above me before sinking into my skull.

The last thought I had was that I didn't want to die with hate in my heart, or betrayal. I didn't want for Peter to do to me what I had done to Terra: left her to die, tricked her into believing that something better could happen to us. And so I gave myself into the truth as the hands bore out my eyes, the pain so vivid that I almost started to laugh: Peter had always known that there was no way out, that nothing and no one would be able to save us. We would never die, but we would never see each other again either. We could go around this place forever, forgetting what it was like to see, forgetting that our bodies had been nothing but toys for others to play with.

ENGLISH LESSONS

"Admonish" is a three-syllable word.

In Japanese, to admonish translates as *satosu*.

To put it another way, the English word "admonish" has three syllables, and so does satosu.

At 7-11, Ayumi is stocking potato chips in the aisles, arranging the shiny pink and yellow bags in a straight row. She stands back to see her work. No matter how many times she straightens them, someone will come and buy them, and then she'll be back here doing it all over again.

She'd learned the word "admonish" as Tao was helping her out with their English homework last week:

Erica's Summer Vacation
    Erica and her family go to the beach
for summer vacation. As soon as they get
there, Erica and her brother start
building sand castles. Their mother comes

over and starts rubbing sunscreen on their faces.

"You have to wear sunscreen!" their mother says, "or else you will get sunburnt!"

"That is true," Erica says. "Last summer, when we went to Disney World, I got burnt very badly."

All day, Erica and her brother swim around in the ocean. Their mother falls asleep on a beach chair. After several hours, she wakes up.

"Oh my gosh! What happened to your faces? They are bright red!" Their mother says, admonishing them.

"We forgot to put on more sunscreen," Erica says. "I cannot believe this is the second time I've gotten sunburnt on summer vacation."

"Well," their mother says. "We will just have to be more careful next time."

"What does 'admonish' mean?" Ayumi asked. The library air was stagnant and damp. The air conditioning unit had stopped working recently, so they'd opened all the windows.

"Like when you tell me that I play too many video games," Tao says. Last week, as they were walking home, Tao had told her to stand by one of the blooming cherry blossom trees so he could take her picture. He'd shown it to her the next day. She looked pale and awkward, her arms too long for her body. *It's a great picture,* Tao said. *A really good one.*

Discounting relatives or school-related reasons, she's probably had only three photos taken in her entire life.

"I heard Maiko saying that she was going to give you something for White Day. And the class president."

"Who cares." He'd looked upset afterward, his words terse as they went through the Q&A at the end. Ayumi had wanted to ask him if something was wrong, but she wouldn't know how to handle it if there was. So better not to ask.

Tao's lips are so red they look like slick cherries. She wants to lick them off.

As Ayumi thinks about Tao's lips, the coy, secret opening of his mouth, she hears her manager's voice.

"Are you even listening to me, Ayumi?" he's asking, arms crossed. "This is the second time this month."

"I'm sorry, sir." She says. She looks back at the potato chips. Someone has already come and bought a bag, ruining her work. She walks over to try and fix them, but her manager stops her.

"Come with me," he says, opening the door to the back room. Through the shut office door, the chimes welcome people as they walk in, buy their cigarettes or sandwiches, walk out. Her coworker Ryosuke thanks them in a cheerful voice, though Ayumi senses how tired he is behind it. Ryosuke recently told Ayumi that he is quitting and moving to Shinjuku. *Come visit sometime,* he'd said. *If you want to make art, you should definitely get away from here. And you definitely need to get away from that creep.*

"I swear I don't know why I keep you around," her manager is saying. He does. Amidst the stacked cardboard boxes, he watches videos on his phone of girls around Ayumi's age. They wear tight swimsuits, gleaming with oil as they jump around on trampolines. They don't have sex; they simply jump up and down, their innocent black ponytails springing from their heads like beansprouts. The manager tells himself he's not a pervert. If he were, they would be having sex with each other.

"I'm sorry," Ayumi says.

The manager sighs, shaking his head in disappointment. She'd worn a ponytail once, and only once. The rest of the time, she wears it down, covering her beautiful young face. What a pity.

"Well, please be on time from now on. Or else I will have to find a replacement."

"Yes, sir," she says. She's not looking at him, obviously thinking about something else. "I promise I will not be late again."

He sighs and gestures toward the front of the store, meaning she can go back to work now, watching her legs move underneath her black slacks. After he's sure she's gone, he opens the video on his phone again. One of them looks exactly like her. Even their legs are the exact same.

Ayumi joins Ryosuke, quickly changing out the rotating chicken skewers and straightening rows of plastic-covered instant ramen. The late-night shift will be here soon, vitamin-deficient and sickly, to take over for them.

"Are you good at English?" she asks Ryosuke as they walk out.

"Sort of." He wipes the sweat off his glistening forehead. If Ayumi were a photographer, she'd want to capture him as he is in this moment: a teenager lacking pretense, his form sharp against the glassy dark. "Why?"

"I have a test next week. Tao is helping me study."

"Ohhh," Ryosuke says, smiling. "I see."

"It's not like that."

"How do you know?"

"He would've said something by now."

"You could always say something, you know."

Ayumi pauses. "I already have."

Two years ago, Ayumi had confessed to him on their walk back home. At first, she wasn't sure if he'd heard her, but when she'd tried to repeat it a second time, he'd stopped her. *Now I have neither happiness nor unhappiness. Everything passes.* And then, *I don't know how to feel.*

"He said that? Oh, God, he's so melodramatic."

"It's a Dazai quote."

"Yeah, and what's worse than a guy who quotes stuff to the person who just confessed to them? Come on."

At the end of the night, Ayumi looks into the store one last time before they start walking. The manager's talking to a young woman, in her mid 20's or so, waving his hands around. His gills flare as he speaks, and when he shakes his head, she sees the glint of silver scales. His head's been like this for weeks now. For some reason, no one else has seemed to notice.

A drunk businessman weaves past her, stumbling into a couple on a date before throwing up in the middle of the sidewalk.

"Watch where the hell you're going, you fucking drunk!" The boy yells. The businessman groans. His vomit is the consistency of the thick syrupy twilight, orange and sweet-looking in a way that makes Ayumi feel like she's about to throw up, too.

Ayumi gets on her bike and pedals away. As the wind stings her face, Ayumi thinks to herself: Pancakes are always best if just eaten with honey and butter, she thinks to herself. No syrup. No way.

"I'm home," Ayumi calls out to her parents. Her shirt smells like french fries. Even at home, the scent of oil hovers in the air.

"Welcome back," her mother calls from the kitchen.

Ayumi takes off her shoes. Her father watches a rerun of an old game show, where the contestants are taking turns hitting each other on the head with blow-up hammers. He turns to face her as she walks in, propping his head up with his hand.

"Ah, Ayumi. How was work today?"

Her father's smile is different. Small black eyes leave no sign of pupils. His face is translucent white, ears replaced by brilliant pink fans.

"It was fine," she says, dropping her bag on the floor, not wanting to make eye contact. "I'm going to go get changed now."

"Your mother is making aji fry," he says as she walks upstairs to her room. "Your favorite." He turns back toward the TV and laughs, but the sound is off. *Glug glug glug.*

Ayumi changes into her pajamas, trying to remain calm. She turns on her computer. "News people turning into fish," she types into Google. The only thing that pops up is a new restaurant where one can take pictures with beluga whale plushies and drink ocean-themed lattes. She searches for around two hours before giving up, her heart beating fast as she curls up in her bed. She gets up again. "Sea lizard pink gills." A number of images pop up in the results, creatures wearing cute smiles on their pink organza faces. It's called an axolotl. Downstairs, her father snores, his short arms leaving trails of slime on the table.

———

Today is the day of the test. All day long, she'd avoided looking up, her neck cramping from gazing down at the floor for so long. But she has to know. Before they start, Ayumi looks over to where Tao is sitting. Rows of sardines and cuttlefish and squid sit slumped over their desks. She stifles a scream. But when she sees him, nothing is different; it's those same lips, the same long, decadent neck. He looks back and gives a slight wave, confused. She blushes and looks down at her desk.

"Okay, everyone," says Ms. Shinohara as she walks into the class. Ayumi holds her breath. She's wearing the same plaid suit as always, but something is different. Her cheeks are swollen, like balloons. Little spikes dart out from every part of her face. Ayumi feels like crying.

"You have an hour to finish. This shouldn't be too hard. If you've been paying attention." Ms. Shinohara punctuates each word with venom. As a teenager, she'd done a homestay in Florida. In her head, Florida is a blur of strip malls, strange and repressed children. The host family had been Mormons. The youngest brother had asked her to have sex with him, and she'd slapped him across the head with a dictionary. None of that same courage remains. Whenever the principal tries to kiss her, she can't do a thing. Who was Sachiko Shinohara now? "Begin."

Ayumi looks down at the test booklet in front of her and flips to the first page.

Erica's Summer Vacation

Erica and her family go to the beach for summer vacation. As soon as they get there, Erica and her brother start building sand castles. Their mother comes over and starts rubbing sunscreen on their faces.

"You have to wear sunscreen!" their mother says, "or else you will get sunburnt!"

"That is true," Erica says. "Last summer, when we went to Disney World, I got burnt very badly."

All day, Erica and her brother swim around in the ocean. Their mother falls asleep on a beach chair. After several hours, she wakes up.

"Oh my gosh! What happened to your faces? They are bright red!" Their mother says, admonishing them.

"We forgot to put on more sunscreen," Erica says. "I cannot believe this is the second time I've gotten sunburnt on summer vacation."

"Well," their mother says. "We will just have to be more careful next time."

Circle the correct answer:

1) Erica's mother got sunburnt.

2) At Disney World, Erica's entire family got sunburnt.

3) This is the first time Erica has gotten sunburnt.

4) Erica's mother says they will no longer go on any vacations.

5) Erica wished that the whole world would sink underwater.

Ayumi reads it over twice. The fifth answer makes no sense. What does that have to do with anything? Perhaps she's just paranoid. The stress of mid-terms has been stressing her out so much, she's started hallucinating. If she goes to the nurse's office, everything will be okay. Even if she has to go to the hospital.

"Excuse me," Ayumi stands up so abruptly she knocks over her chair. Her classmates turn to look at her, their black pupilless eyes boring into her body. "I have to go."

She grabs her bag. Ms. Shinohara yells after her to come back, but she runs through the hallway, bruising her knee against the wall as she flees down the stairs. As she goes to get her bike, she sees one of the younger kids feeding the class turtle. It extends its long, thin neck, swallowing the pellets as they sink down toward him through the murky, green film. A slow smile spreads across the kid's scaled face as he reaches into the tank with gentle flippers.

"Good afternoon," the kid says as Ayumi runs past him. But she doesn't respond. What if this was how people caught it, whatever it was? Her thoughts unravel quickly as she kicks her bike latch and speeds away. Perhaps it is a good thing she doesn't have any friends.

Tao can barely focus on the test. What happened to Ayumi? What's wrong with her? Ms. Shinohara had run outside to get the principal. He can hear them whispering in the hallway before she walks back in, her face pale. She wipes a handkerchief across her beautiful, powdered face.

"I'm sorry, everyone. Please continue."

He finished as fast as he could, placing the booklet on

her desk, taking his phone out of his pocket to text Ayumi. *What happened? Are you okay??*

"Tao." Ms. Shinohara quietly shuts the door and runs toward him, her heels clacking against the wooden floor. "What happened to Ayumi?"

"I don't know."

"She's your girlfriend, right?"

Tao opens his mouth, but nothing comes out. Ms. Shinohara rushes to continue.

"I thought maybe she was sick. She doesn't really do well on exams when she's around people...maybe it would've been best to let her do it solo like she used to."

"I'm going to go now," Tao says.

"Wait." Ms. Shinohara's eyes are filled with tears. "Do you still love me?"

He looks at her. The first time they'd had sex, it had been in that very classroom he'd just left. Maybe it was because she was always complimenting him, maybe it was because he liked the way she smelled: like clean laundry. It had happened so many times at this point, he'd lost count. What was it about him, that always led him to ruining his life? Why was he always running from the things he was scared of confronting?

"No," he says. As he walks away, he hears a small sob escape her throat. It makes him sad, but it also makes him feel...well, he doesn't know how to feel. He never does.

Ayumi dings her bell to move past the old woman walking in front of her wearing a large purple hat.

"Excuse me, ma'am," Ayumi says loudly. She rings her bell again. But the old woman doesn't seem to hear her. She is carrying two large shopping bags from PARCO in each hand. Her arms tremble, her gait slowing until she stops walking altogether. Gently, she sets them down on the sidewalk. After a moment, she takes five steps before setting them down again. Every five steps, the old woman must stop and set her bags down as creatures walk around her, dressed in suits and school uniforms in the sun. Can someone make her stop? Can't she just get on a bus?

Right as Ayumi is about to swerve around her, the woman looks back. Ayumi's heart jumps: She's still a human. And this woman looks exactly like her grandmother. Ayumi freezes, watching her grandmother set the bags down again, shaking against gravity. She's wearing the felt purple hat Ayumi had brought back home from her middle school trip, with the small flower on the side. Ayumi can handle all of this, can maybe even handle it if Ryosuke ends up changing, too. But the apparition of her deceased grandmother is too much.

Without asking, her grandmother pushes herself up on the handlebars, placing the bags on her lap. There is a sea-like smell emanating from her, too, but different than the others—less like pungent, skinned fish, more like ocean water.

"Let's go home, Ayumi," her grandmother says. "Take me home."

So Ayumi pushes off the sidewalk and begins pedaling away. She hears people gasping as she rides by, swerving and ducking between the schools of betta fish, gyarus and the sideways-scuttling businessmen crabs, but she doesn't stop. Her grandmother remains strangely calm, her back straight and dignified as Ayumi rides faster and faster, pedaling as hard as she can. Beads of sweat drip down her face as they go further from the city into the mountainous countryside where Ayumi lives, dense trees lacing over them to shield the sky.

Ayumi knows that logically, the road should be opening now to show a small udon shop to her right, a rice field to her left, familiar houses marking the last five minutes until home. But where the udon shop should be, there is nothing but a milky green sea, a line of stone torii stamped along its middle. She brakes on the small, wooden bridge they have ended up on and her grandmother hops off, hanging the shopping bags from the handlebars before wordlessly turning right. She is walking so fast that Ayumi cannot believe that this was the woman who was struggling to take even five steps just 40 minutes ago.

"Grandma!" Ayumi cries, and tries to ride into the water, but the waves moan and crash against her ankles, making it impossible for her to pedal. She flings the bike away and its red frame sinks slowly into the ocean. Ayumi commands her weighted feet forward where her grandmother's small, hunched body stands unmoving in front of the sanctuary. Ayumi attempts to scream her name again before a huge wave strikes her, slamming into the side of her head. Through her tilted, glasses-less vision, she sees her grandmother waving. Goodbye, Ayumi, goodbye.

When Ayumi's grandmother had started going over to the American missionary's house, Ayumi's parents had pleaded for her to stop. But she had refused. "No one ever comes to see me anymore," she said. Happy to see the guilt in her son's face, she went on to say that it wasn't such a big deal to believe in the Christian God. Jack was a nice man, and he gave her a lot of food and free t-shirts. If this man would stave off her loneliness, the plights of the Japanese nonbelievers was something she could get behind.

Eventually, she'd married him. They'd moved to California together. Ayumi had never forgiven her for that, never forgave her for dying, either. This is the way the world works. You lose the people you think you hate and that mourning lasts forever. Ayumi finally looked through some of her postcards that she'd sent when Ayumi had been younger; all in English. It wasn't until after she was dead that her father had told her that Jack didn't let her speak Japanese anymore.

For months afterwards, Ayumi dreamed in English. Most of it, she couldn't even understand, but they were clogged with it — sentences, phrases, copulas. She'd developed a new hatred, devoted to the language.

Tao had listened to her talk about all of it, watching the soft light reflect on her face, savoring her long pauses as she thought through what she wanted to say next.

Outside of the school, Tao lowered himself into the water, his torso sinking into the waves. He thought about all of the thoughts Ayumi had, all the beautiful things she said to him or to herself: *I like popsicles and the beach. I hate animal cruelty, and I'm glad people don't allow kids to catch goldfish in the pools at summer festivals anymore. I like looking up names of sea creatures. I love Tao, but he doesn't know that.*

He felt ashamed for knowing the last one, wished he didn't. It felt invasive. All his life, for centuries — even back in the day when he was three gods, instead of one — he'd heard so many of these kinds of thoughts that humans had about each other, about themselves. But the more people forgot about him, the more Watatsumi weakened. Eventually, he'd decided to leave it all behind, and eventually, he'd forgotten most of it, too.

But then Ayumi came into his life. Her family had moved next door to his. And the more they spoke, the more he spent time with her, something had begun itching in the back of his mind. He'd figured it all out a year ago.

He wanted so badly to go back to forgetting. As a human, he could love her, take care of her, provide for her; as a god, he knew how selfish it could be to go meddling in people's lives. If she'd known, she might've loved him for different reasons, and he liked how she loved him as Tao. But nothing, not even that which presents itself as eternal, can last forever. There are always rules. Certain things that a god, especially one who's developed emotional ties with a human, cannot ignore.

I want the entire world to drown, she'd said. And this was all that he could do for her.

Ayumi's eyes fluttered open. Bubbles emerged from her mouth. Terrified, she looked down at her body, but nothing had changed. Past schools of mackerel, housewives-turned-horseshoe crabs, she saw an emerald dragon. Why did the look on its face seem familiar? Shy and eager at the same time. The long lashes curtaining its sad yellow eyes.

The mouth. It was the mouth that was the same; though the lips were gone, its familiar shape called to her. She placed a tender hand upon his neck, then drew his head into her arms. She thought about her father, about her mother, about how the world she knew was now gone. The dragon's head shook, as though crying.

"I don't know how to feel," Tao had said to her that day.

And she'd never understood what that meant. For Ayumi, everything was feeling, everything. She traced the mouth, imagining Tao's lips, where they used to be. She realized for the first time that she had no idea how to feel. Sooner or later, she imagined, they would exchange words, he would tell her what it all meant. Isn't that all she'd wanted from him? But there was nothing left inside of her. This mutual emptiness, for now, was all they had to offer.

THE AQUARIUM

You are in an aquarium. Overhead, sharks of all different kinds circle in the archways, their movements swift despite their large, muscled bodies. The tiger sharks and hammerheads and angel sharks all bulleted with pockets of white light. You blink, turn your gaze to your right. An octopus waves at you with its long red arms. You wave back. Next to it is an assortment of all different kinds of seahorses, pink and orange and blue, canvassed by strands of seaweed. Over to your left, schools of small fish dart, frenetic as neurons. You wonder if they know that this is just an artificial recreation of their old homes. You wonder, for some reason, if this ever makes them want to die.

After a while, the fish begin to bore you. You wonder why you came here. Wasn't there something you had to do before this? Like go to work, or go meet someone for lunch...but you don't remember what work is, who you would possibly be meeting and where. There must have been some time before this, you know, but no matter how hard you try to remember, you can't.

So you keep walking, past the children's touch pool filled with sand dollars and stingrays. But something is strange, you realize—there are no children gathered around, no sound save the bubbling of the water and your own muted footsteps as you walk across the carpeted floors.

You are all alone.

You feel panic rise in your chest. Your lazy strides turn into a brisk jog, blurring past jellyfish and their glowing tentacles, glowing cylinders filled with seahorses. Where is everyone? Is there someone you were supposed to meet here, and if so, where are they?

You realize you have been running quite fast. Too fast for a man in his late 30's. You stop to catch your breath. You hear a noise and feel hope—someone else is here!—but it is only an anglerfish, its ugly maw gaping open as it floats inside of its tank. As you sit on the ground, you remember the fact that you must have had a phone, everyone has phones these days (at least, that's what you think), but after checking and re-checking the pockets of your pants and jacket, you realize that there's nothing there.

You sigh, and for the first time in forever, feel like crying. There's a moving walkway right ahead of you, though. You can't see where it leads to, and despite the fear growing in your chest, but there's no use in sitting here doing nothing. You pick yourself up and step onto the walkway. A voice reminds you to watch your step as the belt shakes itself awake.

You continue on for a while, allowing yourself to feel nothing, think of nothing for just a moment. It seems that this walkway has been going somewhere for a long time now. Maybe you should sit again—but suddenly, you feel something wet lapping at your feet. You look down and realize that there is now shallow water rising onto the surface of the walkway. Shells begin to appear in small clusters, pale yellow sand replacing the black rubber underneath. You feel like screaming as you see the water rising fast, rising from your ankles to your calves, but instead the sound remains trapped inside of your chest.

You attempt to run again but cannot, as the water is now at knee-level. You know that despite everything else that seems to have escaped your memory that you are a fantastic swimmer. Regained confidence carries you forward as you quickly remove your jacket and begin to swim. You make quick, even strokes. You're fast. As you continue pushing forward (your body has remembered your age, it seems, and perhaps you were a smoker, because your lungs don't seem to hold much air), you see there is dry surface right ahead of you, lights, and just as the water threatens to swallow you, you push yourself up, gasping, onto the tile.

You do a double take. Tile? You remembered the floor as being carpet. What's more, you're no longer wearing your other clothes. You're in tight blue swim trunks, the same ones you remember wearing as a child. Your balls hurt. The tile is cracked and yellow. You smell mildew as you breathe, the air around you humid and fogged. A vast pool is in front of you, with a lifeguard tower at its lip. Could it be?

Is this the YMCA you frequented as a child?

You still can't remember much, but you remember some things—watching another child dive into the deep end, racing other boys in competitions, even if you don't know their names. But despite your relief that you are finally in a place that you recognize, there are many things that are different, too. Around you are outcrops of coral jutting out from the tile. Anemones wave their spotted fronds. You hear a splash and watch as the enormous humped shell of a sea turtle disappears beneath the surface, sinking into water's skin.

A cold breeze floats through the window. You shiver in your stupid blue trunks, goosebumps lining up across your arms. Toward the deep end, the sprawl continues, dense clusters of urchins and strange trees erupting from the floor until they take over the pool entirely. Eels and sea snakes poke their heads out of the slits a few feet ahead from where you stand. It is not so much beautiful as it is frightening—especially now as the shadows of large, unknowable creatures begin appearing underneath as you jump from one tile to the next, because the floor is shifting, rearranging itself around this ecosystem. The world forces you further into the deep end, and in your heart, you know that it is no longer just the 8 feet written on the wall in crackling black paint. It will be bottomless, a true ocean, and you will be observed by eyes, so many eyes in the murky dark.

You take a look back just to make sure—is that the walkway from the aquarium now stretching toward you, unfolding itself across the water? It stops next to your feet.

To go back to the aquarium, remain on this page.
To remain in the YMCA, go to page 146.

You don't want to know whatever is waiting for you in the water. Maybe if you go back to the aquarium, you can find a phone in there, or an emergency button, some way to call for help. You step onto the walkway and breathe a sigh of relief as it begins to churn forward, leaving the ocean life behind. You put your arms around your knees, trying to calm down.

The walkway stops moving. It tells you to please enjoy your visit to the aquarium. You step off, watching it fold back into itself like an accordion until it disappears.

There's no emergency button on the walls around you. All that you see are two signs, pointing to two different exhibitions:

TURTLE COVE

These fascinating creatures span a wide array of different sizes, shapes, and colors—yet climate change, waste such as plastic and fishing gear, and turtle poaching has made them an endangered species. Our resident sea turtles come from different countries around the world, including Japan, China, Guatemala, Honduras, Australia, Norway, Egypt, Iceland, and more! Come learn about how you can help in saving sea turtles from extinction while looking at some of our favorite shelled friends.

MAKE A SPLASH!

Our famous interactive show features our beloved beluga whale Kaguya. Kaguya's trainers have been with her since she was first born here. As a baby, she weighed 176 pounds. Now, at 55, she weighs a whopping 2,700 pounds! Come see her sparkle and dance while gaining knowledge about all of the different gifts these white travelers of the sea have to offer.

To go to the **TURTLE GROVE** exhibit, turn to
page 150.
To go to the **MAKE A SPLASH!** interactive show,
turn to page 153.
To go back to the YMCA, continue reading.

You decide to keep venturing forward. Who knows what
lies in wait back in the dark rooms of the aquarium? For
some reason, the ocean seems less terrifying now. In fact,
the darkness has dissipated—the water turns clear and
everything underneath becomes magnified.

You gasp as the thousands and thousands of feet below
reveal themselves, all the way gleaming with resplendent
fish and dolphins and turtles making their way through the
corridors of an underwater castle. It is so large that you
can't even see where it ends—the curls of its roof are
encrusted with pearls. Giant squids wrap around the thick
columns leading to the gate. You watch as the squids pull
open the gate doors to let everyone pass through—men
riding on top of golden oarfish, spider crabs with legs eight
times your height scuttling through the sand. Suddenly,
there is a great blast of light, and you flinch away from it.
Your legs slip and you fall from the few shards of tile you
were clinging to in order to stay afloat.

You sink.

No matter what, you can't even attempt to get back to
the surface. The ocean itself is pushing you under, and you
wonder if this is the end. If so, you may not mind it. Life
hasn't been great in a long time. Your thoughts have grown
soggy. You stop struggling, and relinquish yourself to the
deep.

When you open your eyes, you find yourself on the floors of the castle. What's more, two guards float above you with their spears pointed toward your face. You look at their faces and see slits for noses, ears replaced with widespread gills. Their bodies are made of hard, silver scales that end in pointed tails.

"Wait! I didn't mean to come—"

But they aren't interested in talking. You see their tails prick up and the first spear shoots toward your right eye. You allow yourself to scream this time.

You hear one of them grunt. You lower your arms and see that the spear is suspended in an orb. He attempts to tug it out, but it remains stuck. The smaller one seems equally confused as he moves to help him but cannot, as his own arms are encased inside white shackles.

It is then that you see the most beautiful woman emerge from in between them, wearing layers of intricately woven silk robes. You don't believe in love at first sight, but if you did... The yards of flowing black satin that fall from her head just so, streaming behind her as she draws closer to you. Her mouth, the color and shape of ripened plums. Your heart collects heat when she stops in front of you, lifting her gilded fan to her mouth before she speaks (and oh, how her voice sounds so much like the spring):

"Hello, Taro. I've been waiting for you for a long time."

"What?"

You sound so stupid. The guards are still pulling at their spears behind her fruitlessly as she laughs. You can see the soft insides of her throat. Your heart goes thump thump thump.

"You may not remember, but you stayed here with me once. I always hoped that you would come back. Even if you turned back into a mortal, became old, I knew that I would still love you all the same."

Suddenly, she's beside your ear. Her smell is dizzying—you're not quite sure what to call it. Sweet, clean salt.

"Will you stay this time?" She looks up at you and her eyes contain such ache. She grabs at your chest. You feel like throwing up and kissing her at the same time. What should you do?

To stay with the princess, continue reading.
If you decide to decline, go to page 152.
If you want to go back to the aquarium, return to page 144.

For a minute you don't know what to say. Or you do. But it's scary to say it out loud. You do feel as if you know this person from the past somehow, even if you can't remember how or why or when. You just know.

So you say: "Yes."

Her face lights up. That tight feeling in the chest again, the disbelief that such a beautiful person could exist, that you could be the reason for her gladness.

You end up marrying her. Who cares about the past, the parts you don't recall, when your skin touches her skin as you both lie atop a field of anemones, the way she cups your face in her hands as if you are a delicate and precious thing.

Things get bad when you notice one of the ladies in waiting hanging around for you sometimes after breakfast, taking extra care to look at you while setting down your meals. A certain wink in her eyes. You love your wife, you tell yourself. You want your wife. You want the palace, you want the forever, you want to be the man your wife remembers you as—so kind, so loyal, so sweet, apparently, even if he did eventually leave. You want to fuck her without thinking about the lady in waiting with the winking eyes and soft, soft hands that rub your shoulders after a long day.

Eventually hands move down. Shoulders, arms, stomach, dick. Soon you're fucking behind coral reefs, your bodies so flexible in the water, at any point you can both find time.

You really thought you could get away with this forever, huh? You really thought that your wonderful, patient wife wouldn't be able to sense the guilt you feel corroding in your stomach each time you walk back into your bedroom. She always smiles. She always tells you she loves you. She tells you pretty things she noticed that day: Baby beluga. Lost treasure chest that sunk in from above. Sweet grapes falling from their trees in the grove, suspended midair like purple bubbles.

The grove is where she kills herself. The lady-in-waiting cries at the funeral so hard and so loud, so much louder than anyone else, including yourself. You can't find tears. You hate yourself. You hate the lady-in-waiting. You hate your lust, your self-hatred, your desperate need to escape from any sort of commitment in your life.

You never tell anyone, though. Neither does the lady-in-waiting. She kills herself, too, shortly after. You get married to another woman years later. The new princess looks so much like her. Some nights you can convince yourself into thinking it's your dead wife you're falling asleep next to, but then the light falls through the canopy of seaweed in the morning and you smile back. You tell her you love her. You promise to do better this time. You know you will.

Of course you don't.

THE END

If you decide to tell her no, go to page 152.
To go back to the aquarium and choose
between TURTLE GROVE and MAKE A
SPLASH!, go back to page 144.

You decide to go to the TURTLE GROVE. You're not really that interested in the interactive show: Ethics, all of that. You used to love turtles as a kid. Even had one as a pet. Or at least you think you did. Of course you can't remember its name, though. You try not to think about that.

You walk past all the different types of turtles. You learn about the hawksbill, mata mata, flatback, loggerhead, Kemp's ridley.

You pause at the green turtle. For some reason, you like how simple it seems: just green, nothing special or flashy. No cool name.

You smile as he swims up to you. Maybe you're imagining it, but he seems to be smiling back. He even does a little turn inside the water. This makes you laugh. It feels like it's been a long time since you've felt joy, you think, and this little guy seems to know this, too.

Its eyes seem very intelligent, you think, as it glides back and forth doing all sorts of tricks. Every living creature has a soul, you know. Suddenly you feel very sad at the fact that all of these creatures are trapped inside of here. You want to haul the entire aquarium to the ocean, dump them all out into the water.

As you begin to cry, the turtle places one flipper against the glass. It nods knowingly. It is saying, you think, It's okay, I'm happy here, which only makes you cry harder.

Through your tears, you begin to see it shift. Flippers elongate into arms and legs. Shell turns into a straight spine. Hair grows from its bald head, long and soft, until it finishes transforming altogether into a naked woman with her body pressed against the glass.

You step back. You feel an instinctive urge to flee. Bubbles form as she weeps, saying something over and over again.

You watch in horror as she bangs her head against the glass. Harder and harder until her head begins to bleed.

"Stop, oh my God, please baby, stop," you say. In the back of your mind, a question: why did you just call her baby? "Baby, please, don't do this again."

She is out of control, though. She doesn't seem to be able to stop, even if she wanted to. She takes a rock from the ground and begins to make small, perfect slits. The blood is everywhere, crimson ribbons unraveling in the water.

You're screaming at her to stop but she keeps smashing her head against the glass until it breaks. All the water comes rushing out, and the water-soaked woman in front of you is now intelligible, though you wish you didn't have to hear the next words.

"Why did you leave me here. Why did you leave me here? Why did you abandon me? Why? Why? Why?"

It all comes flooding back. You try to grab her arm but she begins to run. You run after her, too, tracing her bloody footprints on the carpet through the aquarium.

You keep running forever. There's no one in the

aquarium but the two of you. No matter which corridor you turn down, you never are quite able to catch her.

THE END

If you decide to say no, continue reading. To go to the INTERACTIVE SHOW, go to page 153.

You freeze as she holds you against her chest. She's murmuring such sweet things still, but maybe if you go back, you can go back to living whatever life it was that you had. Even if you want to stay, you can't.

When you tell her this, she looks heartbroken. She is heartbroken. This beautiful woman who claims to know you is hurting because of you now. You want to hold her so badly. You tell her this. I want to hold you so badly but I know it's not the right thing to do.

She can't stop crying. And then she does something, a small flick of her wrists.

The golden orbs holding the guards in place begin to fade. They grin because they're ready to go.

The last thing you see before you die is her face, so sad even in anger, with an emotion that's something that must be love.

THE END

To choose MAKE A SPLASH!, continue to the next page.

If you want to start again, return to page 141.

You admit that you're interested in the beluga whale. You've never seen one in real life. More importantly, there will be people! You can use someone's phone there. You'll get to return to whatever normal life you had before you got stuck here.

You run fast toward the exhibit. You push the door and oh, thank God, there's light, there's people sitting on bleachers with their kids and cameras, their phones.

The show is just starting. The beluga whale is sitting there smiling serenely at the audience as the trainer throws it fish. It turns over and waves at the trainer's hand motion. The crowd roars with applause.

You run up to a woman wearing a sun visor, sitting next to her kid who is getting popcorn all over the bleachers.

"Can I use your phone?" you ask her, but she shakes her head no, points toward the whale. Goddamnit. You run up to the teenage couple sitting on the level behind her, wearing matching couple shirts. "Hi, sorry to bother you, but can I use either of your phones by any chance?"

But they won't look away from the show no matter how hard you try to get their attention. You run up to more grandparents, lonely people, teachers with their students on a field trip, but they aren't listening.

You have no choice. You just have to watch the show. After that, maybe, someone will let you borrow their phone. You walk with your head pointed down to the very first row of bleachers. If you're going to be here, you might as well get the full experience, right?

The trainer blows the whistle and the beluga whale whips through the air. It dives back into the water with a loud splash. The kids next to you love it. They clap their hands and scream for more. You wish you had a handkerchief to wipe yourself off.

The whale makes a loop before returning to the platform. The trainer blows his whistle, motions for it to do another trick.

It doesn't move. It continues to smile.

The trainer laughs a bit nervously. "Kaguya sometimes has some bad days. But she'll cheer up soon. She loves to make people smile, just like her!"

He throws her a fish. She flicks it away with her tail. He throws her another fish.

She doesn't just smile this time. She laughs. Why does her laugh sound so human?

The trainer is no longer just annoyed, he's angry. "Hold on just a minute, folks. Kaguya seems to be having a bit of a temper tantrum. We'll be back in an hour."

Cheerful music begins to play from the speakers. Everyone groans. The kids cry and stomp their feet. They want to see Kaguya dance. But their parents shake their heads, probably relieved that they get to go home. The crowd begins to walk away but even though you grab at them as they do, ask them to please let you use their phones, they shrug you off. Some of them even look at you like you're crazy, like you're an animal yourself.

You're desperate, though, you need to figure out where the hell you came from, how to get back, and you try to move with the crowd back into the aquarium, but the door slams shut.

A crack sounds through the open air. You turn your head in horror to see the trainer hitting Kaguya with a massive stick.

"You fucking stupid bitch," he screams. He hits her

over and over. "Why don't you ever just do what I tell you to do?" He dumps all the fish in the water, throws the bucket at her head. "You're just a whore. Do what you're supposed to do and give the people what they want. That's your job, isn't it? Just let people look at your disgusting body and laugh. That's all you're good for."

Kaguya doesn't stop laughing, though. In fact, she laughs so loudly it begins to sound like a screech. But the smile is gone. It's a laugh that sounds not just like a warning, but a promise.

The trainer steps back as Kaguya bloats. She's not just 2,700 pounds any more. She must be 8,000. No, more than that. You don't know why that matters right now. Who cares about numbers?

She grows teeth and claws. The trainer looks at you straight in the eye. This is the first time anyone's looked at you this entire time.

"Help me," you hear him say through his microphone. "Help me, ple—"

He's cut off as Kaguya lunges toward him, snapping his spine in half. Beluga whales don't do this. They're usually so calm and quiet. She tears away at one arm and he's still screaming at you to help him, but you don't move at all.

Kaguya looks at you in the eye right before she takes him underwater to drown. You give her a thumbs up. You stand up and clap for her in a way that no one else has probably ever done.

She smiles back through her mouth full of trainer. You watch her spin around in the tank with his limp body and cheer her on. She keeps smiling at you, thank you, thank you for recognizing me as more than just an animal, thank you for wanting me to win, thank you, thank you for telling me that what happened to me was wrong, thank you for reminding me I'm capable of being loved.

At the end, Kaguya dips her humped head back over the surface. Then she turns her back toward you, motions for you to climb on top.

"Get on," she says. "I'll take you home."

And she does.

THE END

THE CHARIOT AWAITS

Josie had tried to unsubscribe from the emails, but they just kept coming. She didn't even know when she had signed up for the newsletter, to be honest. It must have been during her first breakup, the one with the woman who now lived on an artists' compound in Texas, along with two girlfriends and a dog. Josie's dog, to be clear. Josie had looked up pictures of the compound once.

"It looks like a fucking cult!" she had cried to her best friend, Kim, on the phone as she sat on her bed, cradling a large bowl of spaghetti. She didn't even care that she was wearing outside clothes on the bed right now. No one would ever sleep in bed with her or see her ever again anyway. "A fucking cult!"

"What do you mean?" Kim said. "I think you may be overthinking things a bit."

"No, there's like, so many trees. And people smiling really big and looking disheveled and stuff. Oh my God, I bet she's dating the cult leader. The one with the ugly, beady eyes is definitely the leader. I'm sending you a pic."

"Okay." There was a small pause as Kim looked at her phone. "Yeah. Wow. Could be."

"And the other one! The one with the huge tits. I can't even think about it. Is that why she left? Because my tits weren't big enough? Even though they're already pretty big?"

"No. It wasn't the tits. Also, she wasn't really nice to you anyway. You were always complaining about her. How she didn't really talk to you, or insisted the two of you weren't dating for the first nine months of your relationship. Also, when she said it was your fault for being upset when she started dating someone else and didn't tell you. While you were still together, by the way. Do you remember any of that?"

"I *loved* her," Josie sobbed. "*Loooooooved herrrrrrr.*"

"And I'm saying you're better off. Also, please take a shower. Eric told me you said you hadn't showered in two weeks."

"Eric told you that?"

"Yes. Also, sorry, Mae is home so I have to go now. I'll text you later. Love you."

"Okay. Okay. I love you too."

"Please bathe."

Then the phone had gone silent, and Josie had gone silent for three months after that, avoiding Kim, Mae, Eric, her parents, her landlord, the delivery man, her boss at the photo retouching studio. She almost lost her job for that last one. Or did lose it. But she made her way back into her boss's good graces by not sleeping for two weeks to take on more projects, her eyes shot from staring at a screen for hours on end—fixing blemishes, restructuring cheekbones, lengthening and shortening chins, smoothing out the crinkly lines underneath eyes so that these people could go onto covers of magazines and albums and billboards. When she was finally able to sleep again after those two weeks were over, she passed out for forty-eight hours, her dreams rotating images of body parts being rearranged to form perfect bodies, perfect people.

When she got home after work, though, that was when things could get bad.

She had a lot of tarot decks. Around fifty or so. Maybe even more. At first it had been innocent—just something that she liked to collect. She had always loved how different artists drew the cards, their personal interpretations of Strength or Temperance or The Tower, loved that the cards would give you advice that you most likely already knew and could use for personal betterment. Friends gifted them to her on birthdays or even just as a "thinking of you" sort of gift, and if she was wandering through a thrift shop or used bookstore, she would quickly rummage through the spirituality section in search of a deck she didn't own.

But she would never let something like what happened with The Ex happen again. Next time, she would be able to anticipate something horrible like this happening, right? And if she could see something coming in the future that she didn't like, she could change it. Easy. Every decision was one the cards could answer. To get Cheerios or not get Cheerios? To wear this sweater or that one? Should she bring an umbrella to work in case it rained? Would this date be a good or a bad one? Should she go with the nicer mattress that would last around ten years or the cheaper one that would last around three? Should she go outside or not? Any wrong decision could lead to something bad happening, which is why this practice sometimes took up whole nights, Josie staying awake from 8 p.m. to 4 a.m., flipping, shuffling, trying different spreads—Celtic Crosses;

Past, Present, Future; The Year-Long Tree. Ten of Swords.
Two of Swords reversed. Ten of Cups. Six of Wands
reversed. Five of Swords reversed. Each of them compelling
her to keep asking, to not stop until she had arrived at a firm
answer. One that she wanted to hear.

It got to a point where she was even reading during
dinners, at parties, shuffling through things underneath
tables or excusing herself to go read in the bathroom. Josie
could tell that everyone was worried about her, but she just
couldn't stop herself. And it wasn't like she wasn't ashamed
of it either. If she wasn't, why would she do it in the
bathroom?

Finally Kim had intervened.

"I'm coming over."

"Right now?"

"Yes," Kim said, and hung up the phone.

After that Kim had taken all the decks, all the runes,
the crystals and books and everything, and loaded them
into her trunk while Josie cried and tried to grab at things.
Kim just kept shaking her off as she shoved the Aleister
Crowley deck, the Druid Animal Oracle deck, the
Romance Angel deck (the last of the haul) into a trash bag.

"I'll keep them somewhere. I won't throw them away.
Okay?"

"Okay. Okay. Thank you, Kim. I love you so much."

Kim didn't say anything. Then she brought Josie's form
toward her and put her forehead to Josie's for a short
minute. It was very warm.

They stood in the driveway, breathing. Then Kim
moved away, giving Josie's hand one last squeeze before
driving away.

That moment had given her the strength to call a therapist, who helped her work through control issues, letting go,

blah blah blah. Every time she wanted to read, she would write down her worries, a list starting with the very worst thing that could happen and ending with the least catastrophic option. That way she could see if she was being realistic or not.

"Just remember that your mind can lie to you sometimes," Tina would say, as Josie picked at the raw skin on her thumb with her teeth or looked at the floor after revealing something embarrassing or sad about her life. "You don't have to believe everything that it says."

She didn't see Tina as often anymore—maybe once or twice a month. Because now Josie could say she was functioning. If nothing else, she was functioning. She had her apartment that she shared with the roommate whom she wasn't really close with but had known in college, and from whose room she could hear sounds of a controller being mashed late into the night. Sometimes they would see each other in the mornings and ask polite questions about each other's lives before they headed off to work.

She had her neurotic, lanky cat, Terry, whom she loved. She had Kim and Eric and some of their other friends, whom she also loved. Sometimes on her days off, she would walk to the café down the street to order a slice of coconut cake as a treat, eating it by herself as she read through books or flipped through her phone or journaled things like "Today I feel a little bad," or "I passed by a stream today. Azalea bushes growing by it. Very beautiful. I want a better dildo," before going back home.

So yeah, it had all been very dramatic and tiring, for Kim especially. It had taken a lot of work to get this far, to become a semi-stable person with a job and a cat and friends.

But now there were the emails.

The sender was Divine Tarot Guidance. All the subject lines were different iterations of the same thing, more or less.

Don't underestimate this person.

Josie, your true love is waiting for you.

Been thinking about that person from your past again? They're thinking about you too...

Who is this new moon bringing toward you?

And when you opened an email, there was a small, glittering wheel you could spin to get a look into what might happen. After that, you had to pay two dollars to get the full reading.

There it was. That itch. Why not, for old times' sake? Tina had even told her it wasn't something that would just disappear overnight, right? *It's a constant process,* she had said in her calm, measured voice as they sat in her office, Josie crossing and uncrossing her legs on the green velvet couch, Tina passing her some eucalyptus lotion to calm her nerves. *It's hard, but I know you can do it.*

So this meant that it was okay. Just this once.

Josie didn't have a specific question in mind, but she held her breath and pressed the wheel.

It spun for about ten seconds before slowing to a stop.

CLICK TO SEE! appeared in blue cursive, an arrow pointing toward one blurred-out part of the wheel.

And so she clicked.

The wheel spun and spun, a whir of pink as Josie held her breath. The arrow slowed until it landed on a card. *HERE'S WHAT THE STARS HAVE TO SAY ABOUT YOU.* She turned it over, trying not to think.

Six of Cups. On the card was a scene of two children dancing in front of an idyllic garden, a brown fence decorated with weaving white flowers. One of the children was passing a cup to the other, who reached for it with trusting, chubby hands.

Of course Josie knew the meaning of it instantly. Memories, revisiting the past. Something returning. Most people thought of it as being a sweet card, a good card, but Josie had never had a good experience with any of the cards people thought of as good. And this one terrified her. Who was coming back? What did they want from her?

She hit unsubscribe again and waited until she got to the confirmation screen before she slammed her computer shut, trying to take deep breaths and failing as she paced around her apartment. She tried not to think about any people from the past or any people in the future at all. She wanted to never see anyone again, in fact. Okay, this wasn't true, this wasn't true . . . Tina had told her to not do this. The self-isolating.

She picked up her phone and called Kim.

"Hey, what's up?" Kim said. She sounded high, her voice deep and apathetic. But then again, that was always Kim's voice, and Kim was usually high.

"Hey. Um. The stuff is happening again."

"What stuff? Did you get a yeast infection again?"

"No, *Kim*. I take those boric acid supplements you gave me after my period now."

"Oh, okay. Well, then, what is it?"

"It's actually serious okay it's like I'm seriously freaking out can you at least pretend that you care?" Josie spat it out without breathing. She could feel the anxiety screaming inside of her, trying to claw its way out of her throat.

"You don't have to be mean about it. I was just asking." Kim didn't sound high anymore. She sounded hurt.

"Oh. Kim, I'm sorry. I'm sorry, Kimmy."

"You know I don't like—okay, whatever."

There was a brief, hesitant pause. Josie could hear *The Sopranos*, Kim's favorite show, in the background.

"Sometimes . . . sometimes I wonder if you just don't care about me anymore, and it's just nice to have me around, or something."

"No, Kim, I really do love you. I really do. I know I haven't been talking to you as much recently, but it's just because I've been really busy and stressed. You have been and always will be my best friend. I mean it."

"Really?"

"Yeah, really."

There was a brief pause. Suddenly they were eighteen again, at art school, and Josie was forcing her fingers down Kim's throat to make her throw up all the pills she had swallowed after her dad had died, Kim saying *Why won't you just let me fucking die? Why doesn't anyone just let me fucking die?* and Josie had sat there with the wet puke on her fingers until their friend Barry had come running into the painting studio where they were sitting on the tile with a jar of activated charcoal. *I have never seen Kim like that,* Barry said later on, after Josie had put Kim in bed at their house and as the two of them smoked cigarettes on the porch. *Weak, I mean.*

"Thanks," Kim said. "So are you."

"Of course."

"So what is it?" Kim asked. In the background, Tony Soprano was saying, *They think you're weak. They see an opportunity,* to his therapist. The scene following this one featured Tony fucking up one of his crew members on "Bada Bing." She had watched this episode with Kim before—a lot. What would Tony do in this situation? Kim was usually the one who got in fights, but should Josie also beat someone up?

"There's been emails," Josie said ominously.

"O . . . kay . . ." Kim said. "That's normal, yeah? Just put them in your spam folder."

"No, but it's weird. I keep unsubscribing and putting them in spam and all of that and they won't stop."

"Okay. Well, then try to call HQ or something on the website, if you can find it."

"Oh, duh. I'm so stupid. Thanks. Do you want to get Sichuan this week?"

"Yeah, I'm down. Also, wait, what are the emails?"

"It's, like, you know."

"Josie," Kim started to say, before Josie interrupted her.

"Okay! I'm gonna go take care of it, so I'll text you later. And we'll go to HuPo. Bye," Josie said, and pressed the end button as if her phone were on fire.

There was no number to get to HQ. Well, there was, but she couldn't get through to a real person. When Josie tried calling, the automated message on the other side of the line said, "Thank you for calling Divine Tarot Guidance. We're currently busy assisting other light-seekers at this moment. Want to know if this connection is worth it? Then stay on the line and someone will be with you shortly."

"No!" Josie shouted. Oh my God, she was going crazy. She was yelling at the automated voice on the other end of the line. She needed to do something to calm down. Her cat wasn't doing anything. It sat licking droplets of water out of the kitchen sink. Her fern was dying again—it was past the point of salvaging, its brown limbs reminding her of just how embarrassing it all was. How much of a failure her life had become.

I'll prove it wrong, she thought to herself, grabbing a

cup of water and filling it up. *I'm in control of my life, just like Tina said.* She splashed water onto the fern. It looked at her like it didn't care. She was the one who had killed it, after all.

It was too sad to keep staring at it, so instead she tried to make some lunch. Inside her fridge was a pack of Velveeta cheese, a bag of wrinkled grapes, a half-eaten Pop-Tart, and kefir. Maybe she could make some rice and put the cheese on top of that.

Closing the fridge again, she looked at the pictures held on by magnets. There was one of her and Kim from grad school, their faces thin and pale from hours spent in the photo labs or studios. Another was of her and her mother on the Golden Gate Bridge, Josie leaning into her mom's stomach as they held each other close.

She didn't know why she kept that second one there. All it did was make her feel sad. Her mom's smiling face, her long, curly hair; the orange blush she always wore. The way her skin looked, so soft and clear and sweet, before the heroin and the meth.

But on the other hand, if she looked at the picture, she could sometimes feel happy. She could forget about the time when she was eighteen and walked in on her mom fucking someone that wasn't Dad, and her mom saying, "Close the door, Josie. Please close the door, I'm sorry," in a voice that wasn't hers, and for a second, she looked into her mom's eyes and she saw a glimpse of the person who used to be there.

Maybe I should give Mom a call, she thought as she pulled out the rice from the pantry and washed it, feeling the cool water rush over her hands as she scrubbed the rice clean. She could put some money in her mom's commissary, but Josie knew that the more she thought about doing it, the more she would be scared to do so, because she didn't want to hear her mom's voice on the other end of the line telling her how much she missed her, and asking her about her life, and saying how she wished Josie would come visit more often because while she had the letters and the pictures, she sometimes forgot what Josie looked like, and that terrified her. Most of all, Josie didn't want to call one day and hear that inmate #2194 had died.

She put the rice in the pot and covered it. Why hadn't the cards told her that her life would become this? Maybe if she had gotten into tarot sooner, all this could have been avoided. She could have stopped her mom from hanging out with the guy she knew from her job working in Bi-Lo's floral department, and she wouldn't have started using, and then her dad wouldn't have beat the shit out of her mom when he found out what had happened, and then . . . she didn't want to talk about what had happened that got her mom locked up, not really. She didn't feel like sharing that right now, okay?

Her phone rang and she jumped. It wasn't a number she knew, but she decided to pick up anyway. Josie coughed before doing so, because Eric had told her once that if you coughed and said *hello* in a voice that wasn't yours, then you would know if it was a phishing scam because no one would say anything back.

"Hello," she said, in a voice she imagined was dark/deep/threatening.

"Josie?" said the voice on the other end. "Is that you?"

And suddenly Josie felt very dizzy. She saw the rice boiling over and she slammed her hip against the counter to turn the knob. Her cat wasn't drinking from the sink anymore. She was all alone.

"Josie? I . . . I know it's been a while. But it was just . . .
I wanted to see if maybe we could catch up."

Josie didn't say anything, but she didn't hang up either.

The person was silent for a second.

"All I mean is that four years is a long time. And if you
can forgive me . . . I just want to be friends again. I'll always
forgive you, okay? It'll always be okay."

"I have to go," Josie said suddenly. "I have to go right
now."

"No, no Josie, please," they said, sobbing. "Please just
talk for two minutes, that's all I ask."

"I loved you so much and I still love you so much and
because of that I fucking hate you and wish you were dead
so stop just stop don't ever call." Josie was screaming, she
realized, screaming so loudly that she couldn't hear herself
even though the words were coming out. She could still
hear the other person crying when she hung up.

It must have been fifteen minutes that Josie stood there
unmoving after the ex had hung up. She left the rice in the
rice cooker. She walked to her bedroom and sat on her bed.
Her roommate was still awake, playing games. Maybe this
could be the time to ask for a friend, but on second thought,
she knew it wasn't possible.

The Six of Cups. The Six of Cups had cursed her. If
she hadn't started reading again, then this wouldn't have
happened and everything could have been avoided. The
memories wouldn't have come back.

After Josie lay in bed for a while, she got up and walked to
her car. She hadn't bothered changing out of her biking
shorts or her dad's old T-shirt that she had been wearing for
the past three days now. The sun felt so hot on her hair.

Her lips were chapped. It was all so tiring. Still, she managed to pull the door of her piece-of-shit Honda open and back out of the gravel driveway. She went to the bookstore she used to work at two years ago, the place she had bought her first pack of tarot cards from. The owner, Petra, was one of the kindest people she had ever met—one summer, when the fig trees in the backyard bore fruit, Petra had made tarts for Josie to take home. *For you and Kimmy*, Petra had said, patting her hand, because she knew that that week was her mom's birthday, and that Josie had gone to see her the day before and called out of work crying because she wasn't able to handle it. They had been delicious, those tarts, and she loved Petra for making them for her.

The bookstore was a bright blue building that had originally been a house, and its sign hung a little sideways. A small wheelbarrow with hens on the outside of it stood in the front yard. As she walked up the steps, Josie thought again about how this was a mistake. This was most definitely a mistake, but this was just something she had to do. There would always be relapses. That's what Tina had said, after all, right? And if it was her first relapse in a year, then, well, it was okay.

The wind chimes rang as she opened the door. The store smelled of clove and cinnamon, and for a moment she stood there, thinking about the person she had been when she was still working there. And was she even any different now? Maybe nothing at all had changed.

Petra was restocking cards. "Hi, hi, just a second," she said, pulling back her gray hair into a ponytail. Then she looked back and clapped her hands together.

"Oh, Josie! It's Josie!" Petra exclaimed, putting the cards on the floor before running up to hug her. Her hair smelled like chamomile. "Oh, Josie. It's been so long since I've seen you. How are you doing these days?" Behind the counter, Josie saw books that a customer had dropped off: Ferrante, Allende, Bolaño. The name taped to the bag said Sally, a regular who often called in to order Christian CDs and Biblical storybooks. She wondered if Sally ever asked about her.

"I'm doing fine. I missed you, Petra. I . . . I was wondering, um, if anyone had dropped off any tarot cards recently. Maybe a deck we hadn't seen before."

Petra hesitated. Suddenly, Josie remembered the obsessive way she had stared at the computer at work, constantly refreshing different websites where she could get free rune and tarot readings. Petra didn't say anything, and that was part of what made her so ashamed—that Petra pitied her.

"Are you sure that's a good idea?" Petra asked, gently.

"Oh, you know. I was just feeling nostalgic. How are the grandkids?" Josie suddenly felt the need to change the conversation, and quickly. She looked at the table with the new books on it and picked up a small paperback with a black cover. "I'll take this one."

"They're fine," Petra said as she rang her up, gently placing the book in a brown bag. "Lia asks about you sometimes. She said she liked it when you two read books together."

"Tell her I say hi."

"I will. This is a good one, by the way. You'll like it."

"I'm sure I will."

"Come by some time, all right?"

"Yes, of course. I promise. I do need to go now, though, I'm sorry."

"Oh, no worries, no worries," Petra said as she ran

Josie's card through the POS system. "I understand. Busy life, doing all that design work that you do."

"Thanks for everything, Petra," Josie said, and she meant it.

"Of course, Josie. Anytime."

It was only after waving to Petra a couple of times and getting to her car that she saw that Petra had still given her the 30 percent employee discount, with a small pressed flower tucked inside. She didn't even know what book she had picked up, but when she turned it over, she saw that the title was *Signs Preceding the End of the World*.

How fitting, Josie thought. Then she drove to the grocery store.

Desperate times called for desperate measures. Josie shook a pack of Marlboro Reds out of her pocket and lit one in the parking lot before she went in, stamping it out with a wet boot as a slow drizzle started forming around her. Once inside, she bought cloves and cinnamon, a pig's tongue, a yard of black twine, some paper, black pepper, rosemary, and red chili powder. She kept her head low at the self-checkout line, feeling as if somehow the people around her would be able to read her thoughts. She pulled her hood over her head and ran through the rain.

Once back at her house, she did what she remembered how to do. First, she made the salt circle in the correct way —clockwise, three times. She got up from the floor for a minute to get a candle from the kitchen, then anointed it with olive oil, slowly massaging it from the bottom to the top. After that, she rolled it around in the rosemary and some calendula that she had found sitting at the top of the pantry. She carved all the runes she could think of onto it—

Thuriaz, Sowilo, Isa, Nathuriz—with her old dagger, which she had retrieved from its spot beneath her record cabinet.

She carefully wrapped the pig's tongue with black twine. Then she filled a jar full of oil mixed with the black pepper, the red chili, the cloves, and the cinnamon. Josie didn't care if someone passed by the window and saw her right now. "You can't speak to me, you can't speak to me," Josie whispered as she held the flaccid weight in her hand, wet and heavy with blood. "Shut the fuck up. Shut up. You can't call me again." She kept repeating these words as she dunked the tongue inside the jar and quickly thrust it underneath the kitchen sink.

She could hear her roommate singing in his room, some pop song from the early aughts that she recognized but couldn't put a name to. Suddenly, she felt terribly lonely.

Josie picked up a bag of cat treats and shook them. Terry came galloping toward her, and as he lapped the surface of her palm, she stroked his glossy black fur. "What would I do without you, Terry?" she whispered. Because the fact of the matter was that if Josie were to let Terry out now, release him into the wild, he would be fine. He would learn how to survive and maybe even forget about her after a while, settling into his new home somewhere among the trees.

She wanted to punch something like she had when she was younger, but this wasn't what Tina would have wanted her to do. She found a pen and stabbed it into her thigh. Blood leaked out of the small hole.

She sat at her desk, Terry purring on her lap. As the blood soaked through her bike shorts, she started thinking again. What exactly was it that she wanted so badly to avoid?

She couldn't help it anymore. She found some images

of decks online and printed them out on construction paper. This was more accurate than any other system, to do it physically. After they were done printing, Josie cut them out and quickly shuffled them, her heart beating fast.

What do I need to know, she asked the cards. *That's all. I just want to know what's going on. What do I need to know. Please.*

She laid each one down, and with each overturned card came a sense of horror. She looked at her spread laid out on the floor.

It made sense to her now. Unfortunately, it all made perfect sense.

"I didn't mean to," Kim sobbed. "I didn't mean to do it."

"You did. You never cared. You didn't care about Mae's feelings, or mine. Jesus fucking Christ, Kim, does Mae even know?"

High Priestess. Seven of Swords. What was going on? What had really happened between the two of them? That was the first thing she had asked when Kim had picked up.

"You know I wouldn't do something like that to you, Josie. You know I wouldn't, you know I wouldn't—"

"Stop. Just stop," Josie said. At this point, she couldn't feel anything: not rage, not sadness. Just numbness. "You fucked her, didn't you? I knew it. I knew you did, and I pretended you didn't. You acted like a fucking stupid slut who doesn't care about anyone but yourself. You've only ever cared about yourself. You're just a burden, to everyone. Remember that time when me and Eric had to stop you from offing yourself? And you act like *I'm* the one who needs help? Ha ha. Everyone's so tired of you. I'm tired of you. You were right. Oh, also, did you help upload my pictures onto that site too?"

"Josie," Kim said, sobbing, but Josie didn't care anymore.

"Put Mae on the phone," Josie said. It felt so good to be angry. It felt so good to finally not be weak. Blood was rushing to her head and she realized she could barely see. "I know they're probably right there. I want to tell them just exactly what kind of slut they're with. You probably haven't even told them."

Josie smiled to herself, her entire body pulsing. Kim's sobs faded as Kim passed the phone to Mae.

"Josie," Mae said calmly. "There's something you should know."

What had it been that she so desperately wanted to avoid again?

"Sure, whatever," said Josie. "Let's hear it."

Josie was sitting at the dam that crossed the river. As a kid, she and her mom would sometimes come here and search for crawfish, though they never found any. There had been some boys catching them, and Josie had wanted to do it too. *Do you think you could help us?* her mom had asked, but Josie tugged at her hand and forced them to leave. As they walked across the grass, she told her mom that she didn't care anymore about any damn crawfish. All her mom ever did was embarrass her.

She would never forget the look on her mom's face when she said that, her curls falling over her face as she glanced downward like a chastised puppy. Why had her mom been ashamed? It was Josie who was the asshole. Her mom had tried her best. She always had.

Was this what the cards were trying to tell her all along? *Look*, she wanted to tell the universe. *It isn't my fault, okay? Can you get that through your fucking head?*

She pulled up the HQ number for the tarot website again. She immediately got through to someone this time.

"Hello," a voice said.

"Hello, yes. How are you?"

The woman laughed. Her voice was so soft and warm and lovely. Josie felt calm now, so calm that she felt as if the last forty-eight hours had never happened.

"Oh, I'm great, Josie. How are you doing today?"

"You know, I'm not doing so well. I found out that my ex had been cheating on me for three years. And Kim had walked in on her once at this guy Eric's house. You know what's fucked about that? Eric was Kim's and my friend. And Eric made Kim promise not to tell me, because I would lose my mind. Because everyone knows I'm psycho. Ha ha.

"Mmm," the woman said. "That is just so hard."

"And you know the reason Kim tried to kill herself was because of what happened to her as a kid, right? Her dad doing that disgusting shit to her for years and years and years. She tried to kill herself a lot of times, actually. But I was horrible. I could've guessed it. I did guess it. Eric had tried to tell me something but I walked away in the middle of him talking to me. Ha ha. And years later I read these cards and I thought that what they were saying is that Kim had fucked my ex like a slut and was hiding it from me. So I was so angry. I called and I was so, so angry."

"Right, of course. That's very understandable, to be so angry," the woman said.

"I'm going to kill myself. Not Kim. Kim is good. Kim has always been good to me. Just myself."

"Mmm," the woman crooned again, "that's so awful to hear. Everyone knows how much you love Kim, Josie."

"It's just that she was my best friend, and I didn't mean to say such awful things to her. I didn't mean any of it. Doesn't she know how much I love her?" Josie was crying now. She hated how much she was crying.

The woman started crying along with her.

"She knows. Of course she knows. You're doing the right thing, Josie."

"Thank you so much. I love you, too. Even if you're just some person."

"Thank you, Josie. When are you coming to visit?" Suddenly the voice turned into her mom's.

"Mom? Mommy? Is that you?"

"Yes, it is. Oh, and your ex is here too. I always loved having her around the house. She was such a help, you know?"

"Yeah, she was. She really was. Maybe she wasn't such a horrible person after all, right?"

"Kim wants to get on the phone now," her mom said. Josie waited as she passed the phone to Kim.

"The right thing to do is not always the right thing. You're listening to your mind right now, aren't you?" Kim said, and for a moment Josie could see Kim in her mind's eye—the freckles stamped across her nose like stars, her broad face and watery brown eyes.

Oh, Kim. You'll never know how much I loved you.

Before Josie could say this, though, a car showed up nearby. Josie squinted away from the bright white headlights.

"It's past curfew, young lady," the man in the uniform said. "Isn't it about time you went back home?"

"Who's going to take care of Terry after I'm gone? Will you take care of him for me?"

"Excuse me?"

He glanced down at her hand and saw the dagger, the blood pooling from her arms and throat, her hair scraggly and wet, her clothes the same ones she'd been wearing all week as she crouched like a gargoyle near the water.

"Hey, are you alright? Are you alright? Why don't you give me that, and we can get you to a safe place," he said softly.

But she knew what safe places looked like, and she knew that him speaking into his radio wasn't what he was saying to her. Everyone lied. Everyone left, or lied, or they were hurt by people she thought she could trust. Josie lied and left and hurt people, too.

"Alright, I'm going to ask you to drop that now, little lady," he said.

A muffled voice came through the radio, staticky and small.

They were on their way, and they would do what they had to do.

Josie knew destiny when she saw it. She grabbed the dagger and, slowly, pointed it in the cop's direction.

"I loved those fig tarts," she said, and ran toward him laughing, her teeth and the knife glinting in the dark, the river and the crawfish inside of it laughing alongside her. Destiny was beckoning and she followed it, her limbs becoming liquid, becoming water.

DUCKLING

It had been months since she had touched me. Whether she had another lover or not, I didn't know, although I could have found out easily—a quick look into her eyes when she would come to my house straight from work, her whole body smelling of camphor. A peek into the photos on her computer, if she chose to leave it overnight, as she sometimes did when she decided to stay for two days in a row. I knew the password because she kept it the same for everything-ATEVA004!- and I knew this password because she trusted me with it. She trusted me with everything—money, watches, bills, time. So what right did I, her chosen confidant, have to doubt her?

Her official title was "Topical formulation scientist," mixing and measuring and melting ingredients to make pain ointment for a famous Chinese company. The work was not enjoyable for her; monotonous, uncreative. At night as I tucked my head into the crease of her armpit, she would tell me what she really wanted to be: a perfumer, developing all the different scents she wanted instead of the same sharp, cold medicinal smell.

The beauty of fragrances, she told me as I stroked the side of her cheek, her stomach, all the parts of her I could touch, was that they came alive in different ways on everyone's skin. It all depended on the person wearing them. Sometimes, she would make small vials of scents for me— saving the leaves of the tomato plants that grew wild in the field behind the factory, plucking blossoms from the yuzu trees in people's yards as she walked from the train station, saving discarded orange peels from the compost, boiling these down into different oils for me to smear across my neck, my wrists, the backs of my ears.

Truth be told, I didn't care much for them. I wanted to smell like myself. Like nothing. But I appreciated the gestures for what they were—offerings of love, or something like it, I told myself, and so kept them in small vials, each labeled with the date she had given it to me and the ingredients they contained in the bottom of my dresser.

If I thought about it now, though, it had also been a long time since she had given me anything like this either. Lately our evenings were as they had been when she first came to me—hours of us clawing at each other, our moans low and desperate as we bucked against each other's wet lips or fingers or pussies. But we didn't speak. Even if I tried. Even though I did try.

Maybe it was true that she knew my secret, had heard the rumors, and that was why she had responded to me the way she did at the grocery store when I asked if she would like to spend time with me one day.

Up until that point we had only known each other in passing—brief chats at our friends' parties about what we did, our shared interests, small spurts of conversations underneath which I hoped she couldn't sense my desperate longing. One night she had stretched her leg across mine at a club as our friends danced, drunk and illuminated by the purple lights, the clouds of white smoke. I felt like I was going to die if I looked at her so I tried my best to keep my eyes straight ahead, staring at our friend Jiani as she shrieked and spun and kissed different strangers around her. I managed to work up the courage to look at Min, both fearful and hopeful that she would be looking at me with desire, or anything really. I could have done with anything. But instead, she was just looking at her phone, her other hand combing through her hair as if she were distracted.

I didn't know what to do with the leg on top of mine, wanted to touch it but was anxious this would be the wrong move, so I floated my hands above it for a second before I settled on pretending I was on my phone as well. I felt terribly embarrassed and awkward. I told myself the next day it probably didn't mean anything at all.

But at the grocery store, when I had seen her in the dried food section picking out packets of squid and plum, I had asked her anyway. Would you like to go out with me sometime? I said. I forced myself to look at her face when I said it.

Of course. I've wanted you for a long time.

Those were the words she used. She had smiled at me, the dimple on her right cheek showing, and I had felt my face burning as we exchanged our messaging accounts.

Later, when I went home, I repeated those words in my head, rearranged them into different sentences until I fell asleep.

Wanted me? Did want mean sex or love? Did that mean the leg incident had been real? A long time—how long was that? If she used the word "want" instead of "like" did that mean she only wanted me because she wanted to have sex with me?

Anyway, it didn't matter. I thought about her leg on top of mine in the club, then what she looked like underneath the tight-fitted black pants she had been wearing that day, then I thought about her lifting my legs above her shoulders and making slow motions with her tongue on my clitoris, around it. I was so lost in the fantasy that I surprised myself that when I came, I moaned her name out loud. It was such a shameful thing. What right did I have to say her name like that?

But that was then and this was now.

She opened the door, which I now left unlocked most nights so that if she needed to get in, she could. She knew the passcode for the building, how to get through the gate as well. Walking to the kitchen after giving me a brief hello, she grabbed some boxes of food out of the refrigerator and turned around to heat them up on the burner.

When she saw me, she dropped everything. The pan, the pork, the eggs, the vegetables, all of it smeared across the tile.

"What did you do to yourself?" Min asked. I couldn't tell if she was happy or horrified. "What did you do?"

"What you wanted me to do," I said. I glided across the floor and kissed her. After a moment, her lips kissed me back. Soft at first, then harder and harder until it seemed like we were trying to swallow each other.

First I became a cloud-woman. Min had always liked watching them as a child, one of her only good memories from that period. Laying on the grass with her father, pointing out their shapes in the sky.

I lifted up my skirts, let her lap up my water. Her mouth was covered in dew when I kissed her. When she slipped her fingers inside of me, she muttered, *Fuck. You've never been this fucking warm and wet before.* I went down on her and my tongue was so soft, like dragon's beard candy, she actually cried from how good it felt. I absorbed her smell, her sticky residue like a sponge inside of me. It felt good to hold this much.

Next, I became a piano-woman. Min used to love to play the piano when she still had time, making up beautiful songs that no one had heard except for me, and even then, only a few selected ones. Not even half of the melodies she composed. Her fingers ran over my keys, which had taken my ribs' place, as she fingered me from behind. Each time her fingers pushed inside of me it was like she was playing again. Music pouring out of me, her music. Again, she wept. I cradled her in my arms afterward, petting her head, kissing her face. The first time she ever allowed me to do something like that.

I was a flower-woman. She loved how I smelled, like hibiscus, like lavender, like roses. Some of the names I didn't know, flowers I had never seen, so I had her describe them to me. She squeezed my buds until they blossomed, burst, my pollen everywhere, all over her face, the bed, our bodies. We went through a flower encyclopedia afterward, and she pointed out her favorites—peonies, chrysanthemums, orchids—and told me why she loved them. Their curving stems, their large, pink faces.

I was a sea-woman. I was a book-woman. I was a honey

and a fruit-woman, too. I loved slipping under her tongue like a secret, and I loved the way her body slid down the corners of whatever body I had. Whatever she wanted, I became. I was learning so much about her I had never known before. It didn't matter if I disappeared.

Eventually, of course, she wanted me to change back. She said she missed my face. She said she missed spending time with the real me. Going out to bars, passing time with our small jokes, the way I used to talk to the food as I cooked it in order to make sure it was delicious.

I had to explain to her, then, of course there were rules to this. And the rule was that each time I changed, I would have to have someone remind me of myself in order to morph back into that form after everything had ended: Your hair is dark black. You are very tall. You don't like mung bean. You are scared of heights. You were from a city that you never went back to after age 18. Things like that.

She couldn't believe it. Her body kept twisting as she screamed with despair, rocking back and forth as she held herself like a temperamental child.

Why didn't you tell me? Min asked. *Why didn't you say anything beforehand?*

I was, of course, another woman now. I had taken the shape of her dead ex-girlfriend—plump lips, sharp bob, beautiful smile. Her final request. Mei Xiang, dead at 20 after a car accident. Her first love. It had made me so happy. Finally, she would want me.

I wrapped a hand around her shoulder as she wept, called her the nickname she had told me Mei Xiang always had—"little duck," because of the way she walked. I was beautiful. I was perfect. I was what she wanted, and she would realize soon that my original core was just a disgusting thing that we had disposed of, together.

"It's okay, little duck," I said, kissing her eyelids as she began dozing off to sleep, tired out from all the tears. Soon it would be time for another work day, and she would return to me every night as she had done for the last month. Everything was so beautiful. "It's okay, it's okay."

A MOTHER'S LOVE

It happened at the train station. I was twelve and my mother was still young, thirties, maybe. The wind was peeling the skin off of our nostrils in the way that it does, especially, in the wintertime. In our arms we carried groceries: carrots to stir into stews, packaged slabs of lamb, two large grapefruits. A huge vat of Vaseline collected lint and lipstick stains in my mother's purse.

"Here," she said, handing me a packet of tissues as I tried to blow snot onto my sleeves without her noticing. She didn't criticize me, which was strange, considering how she was always talk talk talking about what I had done wrong that day, and if not that, about how she should have married her Swedish boyfriend back in the eighth grade and not my stupid, useless, clown of a father, and if not that, then about the state of her cuticles and bunions, or.

I blew my nose into the tissue. It was decorated with small pictures of a cartoon mouse, whose voice I'd always hated. Peeking up at my mother, I thought about asking her if something was on her mind, even if I didn't really care. She was too busy gnawing on her thumb to notice, gnawing the tip of it away with her teeth, a tic I hadn't noticed before. Small circles of skin collected at her feet, dusting the tops of her sensible white shoes.

"Mama, you're bleeding." I spoke before I could stop myself, and I winced away from the inevitable backlash that was coming.

Instead, she kept on chewing, eyes diseased with a strange brightness, soft gurgles of pleasure erupting from somewhere deep in her throat. Blood flecked the collar of her coat. I wanted to scream but I knew in the back of my mind that I couldn't or that something awful, just awful, would happen if I did. The pack of cartoon tissues dangled forgotten at my side.

"Come on," Mama said, pulling me onto the train. Her voice wasn't that of a monster's or even my mother's. It was sweet, vulnerable, like the underbelly of a cat.

We sat on the cushioned seats reserved for the ill and elderly. The train wheezed its way back into motion, the passengers around us asleep or busy with their novellas. Nobody glanced our way. One man reached into his coat to pull out the remains of his roast beef sandwich, tenderizing the meat with too-white veneers. Hot smells of blood and mustard traveled throughout the car, making me want to vomit.

I stared straight ahead of me, shaking. Only five minutes we had been on the train and yet my mother, having successfully swallowed her thumb, had now jammed the whole of her hand into her mouth. She made impatient, wet noises as she ground up the painted acrylics of her nails, hacking and spitting as splintered bone caught her throat. I am helpless, I thought, and I begged the rest of the passengers to notice me, to alert me about what I should do, and yet they did nothing. One teenage girl met my desperate eyes and smiled sweetly before turning back to her friend to discuss the newest trend in fashion technology, where they had discovered a shade of pink to weave into clothing that brightened or dulled depending on how romantic a person was feeling that day.

We arrived at our stop. "Please carry the groceries," my mother said, as she no longer had arms, her shoulders gristly underneath the remains of the purple blouse she had picked out this morning, fluttering down the stairs to prepare coffee and wheat toast for Papa, with his high blood sugar and intolerance for frills, before he left to visit his mother in a neighboring town. A man entering the train bumped into us as the doors opened and we passengers came spilling out. "Pardon me," he said to my mother, tipping his hat as he hurried by.

The street to our house was dark now, peppered with white frost. I had never once cried out to my mother as a young child, preferring the attention of my father, but now I craved for her love, the too strong touch of her hands as they braided my hair, the attentiveness to small details such as my untied shoes and jam-stained clothes. *Mama, mama,* I wanted to cry. *Look at the snow, Mama,* but she was so many steps away from me, hurrying along the sidewalk as if fleeing, her mouth working around her right shoulder, flapping like a trout's. I could barely see her figure any more, and my arms had grown tired from carrying the bags of groceries.

I was exhausted and frozen when I finally reached the door of our house, panic fogging up the corners of my mind as I gently pushed the door open with my foot. The house mirrored the outside world: bleak, silent, black, but when had it not? I had known since my childhood that this house was one ruled by fear. My father, a large man, slept on the couch most nights, a thin blanket covering his feet as the TV played on. It was from him that I had first learned the meanings of sadness and fear at such a young age.

"Don't bother your mother. She's not feeling well today," he would whisper as he woke me up for school, my eyes still unfocused, the world continuing my dream around me.

"Why?" I would ask before I knew that the question was pointless—that there was never a reason for her silences, the way she would travel large distances in her mind amid conversations. "What's wrong with her?"

"It's nothing, honey. She probably just ate something a little bad last night," he'd said cheerfully, but in the moment before he pulling my shirt down over my eyes and onto my body, I would see that same question inside of his pupils: Why didn't she love us? What had we done wrong?

I would observe her quietly as she did her makeup in the living room from the corner of my eye as my father spooned porridge into my bowl for breakfast. She would slather lotions and eye creams on to the pale, smooth surface of her face and then dip different brushes into reds, pinks, and corals until she looked like a painting of a sunset. *I want to be that beautiful*, I would think as my father and I scraped at the excess in our bowls. His face was a large, bulky nose that I had inherited, heavy eyelids and brutal eyebrows that matched mine. I loved him, but he was a shipwreck, not a sunset. It bothered me that we looked so much alike.

So once, during a day I spent at home alone due to a cold, I tried to imitate the sun. I stuck my stubby fingers into a cold, wet cream and smeared it across my face. I worked eyeshadows into the creases of my eyes and all the way up to my temples, drew uneven lines of black across them as a finishing touch. The elegant, Japanese-made brush handle felt awkward in my hand as I stippled it across the cream blushes, scalding my cheeks in the violent reds. And last came the lipstick, which glided with surprising ease across my wet lips, the feel of it like water.

I looked into the mirror and saw myself a boy blurred, a ghost of a woman melting into my reflection. The makeup was terrible, and yet I felt significant but also scary—why did I look so much like my mother? It couldn't be that I had succeeded in my attempt; rather, I looked farther away from her than ever. And then I saw what she must have seen every day in the mirror, which was a monster trying to force itself into human form, the disguising of a naked shell so that it resembled a bright Easter egg.

The front door had opened, but I'd remained seated, unable to move in my fear. I'd heard my mother's footsteps grow closer before suddenly stopping. I forced myself to turn and face my punishment.

There was a look of triumph on my mother's face. Her chest rose and fell in heavy breaths as we gazed at each other. It wasn't until later that I realized she had been rejoicing in my suffering: I had become a miserable worm like herself, trying to masquerade as a butterfly. We never spoken of the incident again, but after that, my mother had taken care to move her vanity into her bedroom, a place I never dared to enter.

And now, my feet damp from the snow, a soft glow of light pulsed like an erratic vein from that living room where I had tried to make myself anew. I knew that she was there. Dropping the groceries on the floor, I forced myself to look inside. There, past the furniture and tangle of shoes and history books, sat the head of my mother, tongue desperately lashing out to find the taste of skin, an animal of its own. Yet it was the eyes that frightened me the most, the perfect serenity in them as they looked up at me from the ground, so similar to the look she had given me in the past.

PLEASANTRIES

On the way to Minnesota, I'm forced into conversation with the stranger next to me. It's a 12-hour flight. The girl is from Delaware, or Connecticut, some state I don't care about.

She is studying worship leadership at a Christian college, she says, and waits for me to give indication of approval.

"Well," I say. The flight attendant is making her way down the rows with little cans of soda and bags of pretzels. She wears kitten heels on her feet and antlers on her head.

"Merry Christmas," says the flight attendant. "Pretzels or cookies?"

"'Tis the season," I say. "I'll take the cookies." She hands me a biscotti broken clean down the middle.

"Are you a believer?" The girl next to me wants to know as the flight attendant leaves.

"I'm pretty tired. So I think I'll go to sleep now."

I turn away from her, rest my head against the hard plastic of the window. I don't want to be impolite; it's true I want to sleep. The thought of her sadness makes me anxious, but I command myself: Sleep! Right when it's about to happen, she taps me on my shoulder.

"Excuse me. I shouldn't have asked that question."

"It's quite alright," I say. I'm relieved despite my tiredness. I want to eat my biscotti, and look outside the window toward the rain. I want to know nothing about the place I've come from or the people I knew there.

I unwrap my biscotti and eat it. As I'm chewing, she tells me about how she is a believer not because of any kind feelings toward God; no, quite the opposite. She hates God and finds him unbearable, but knows nonetheless that he exists.

"So why the singing and the guitars?" My mouth is full and the biscotti is dry as I try to swallow it. I realize I've forgotten to ask for a drink, so I push the button above my head. The reindeer comes back. One of her antlers droops.

"I'll just take some water please."

She hands me the water.

"Merry Christmas." I say it first this time so she doesn't have to. She smiles. Maybe, most likely, it was just for my benefit. I of all people would know how much the sad must suffer for those around them. We tell them we are fine or that we are making progress, or we smile at the idiotic things they say. And they think us liars, just as they should.

The flight attendant heads toward another glowing button. I turn toward the girl again.

"Please continue," I say.

"I thought you were annoyed."

"Yes. A little. But I also love a good story about hatred."

She purses her lips and looks around my face, at the air.

"What are you doing?" I ask.

"Reading your aura."

"What does it say?"

"It says you bear the curse of the beast. No, not really. It just says that you're about as normal as the rest of us."

She reaches into her bag underneath the seat in front of us. While our voices haven't been very loud, I'm worried they will carry and we will absorb the ill will of veterans and babies, nurses and graphic designers. So when she shows me her book, I lower my voice this time so that only the two of us can hear.

"Why this book?"

"Oh, because I hate it. It's the worst book I've ever read."

"'Liu Cixin's *The Three Body Problem*, translated by Ken Liu.' I'm not much of a reader. What's to hate about it?"

"Oh, everything," she says. She licks her finger, a tic I thought was mostly made up, and turns straight to the page she wants. "But here's a great line: 'But burning was their fate; they were the generation meant to be consumed by fire.'"

Neither of us speak for a while. We enjoy the stale, cold air as it touches our faces to death. I try to think of the last book I read, but then give up.

"Being a prophet does sound like a difficult job." I'm not lying, it does sound difficult. To have faith and negate that faith by virtue of who you are. But I don't think she is one. I've met my fair share of them. They are somber and quiet people, and many of them were my lovers once. I liked to hear them warn me of my life, my fatal choices, but it does take a toll on one's heart to love those whose ears are attuned to god. The last one said she imagined life like a slipper: something one could pull on or off at will. We had sex once or twice. She liked to chew on bits of plaster due to her anemia. She married a gymnast who had muscles on top of his muscles. I wondered if he'd grown more of them since, muscles quadrupled.

"I'm less of a prophet. More of a masochist."

"Are you Chinese?"

"Yes, are you?"

"Yes."

"Let's please don't talk about our mothers making dumplings."

We shake hands.

The plane pushes forward into icy Minnesota. I realize that I feel a sense of unloosening inside of me, my fear turning my body into a locust or a very fraught knife. The remembrance of the dangling antler, the deep sorrow of not knowing the book this girl hates or what book I've read in recent years causes me to sob. I put my hand against my mouth.

The girl turns again toward me, and says:

My burning happened at age 6. We went camping in my backyard, even though that's not camping at all, and I leapt into the fire pit: or more accurately, the fire pit leapt into my leg. I remember the shock before the pain. My father, a doctor, did nothing to save me, only stood. My mother and grandmother iced my leg down. We took down camp. I've been wanting to burn all my life, do you understand? That's why I'm going to Minnesota. I want to die to laugh at God, and I know, yes, I know, that is why you are here as well. We sat down because of our shared fates, and we won't be talking about our mothers or dumplings; mine didn't make dumplings, she's allergic to gluten. My mother accomplished death, it's a normal occurrence, so why do I find it so unbearable? Perhaps it was the fire pit, anger over the fact I'd felt such intense pain before I became its true owner. If I hadn't been burned that day, would she still have killed herself? I am trying to say that neither you or I can die. You have the eyes of someone who lives forever despite not wanting to. There are nine more hours left on this flight, and that's more than enough time to save ourselves, shall we fall in love?

Her face returns to her. She finds my hand and holds it. In the front, a group of missionaries begins to sing of the Lord and Savior Jesus Christ. The girl sings along with them while laughing. Her sin is honesty, which breaks down into purity. Inside her palm, my hand gleams. The flight attendant's antler stands upright, like an antenna pointed south.

(_____)

(Male 1) feels (_____) about the fact that he will shoot a man tomorrow in (___). Or rather, he was feeling (_____) about the fact he would never be able to see his wife again. Just for one last time, (Male 1) wished he could place her tender (_____) nipples in his mouth again, and hear her (____). He felt himself growing large underneath of his tight (_____) pants. (Male 1) feels sick at the thought (Woman) could be fucking (Male 2) right now. He finishes his cigarette, flicking it out of the (_____). The voice in his head repeats a single phrase: (_____, _____).

(_____), (Male 2) screams after (Woman) tells him about her husband's knowledge of their affair. He screams, not because he is (____), but because he is (_____).

"(_____)?" (Woman) asks. Her face looks (_____), and as she cries, she appears to (Male 2) like a pillar of ash. Like a (_____) memory, foreign and unimportant.

"No," (Male 2) replies.

"Will you tomorrow?" (Woman) asks. She is holding onto the door frame, her nipples protruding from her shirt. (_____) Is falling behind her outside the window. Now she is no longer a (_____) memory, but a still from a portrait. She appears to him as beautiful as the day when he first met her, a short woman the size of a (_____), shivering outside of the train station in her (_____) dress.

He'd never wanted to sleep with her. But she had kept following him, telling him she was a (_____) saleswoman and brandishing vegetables at him that she pulled out of her infinite bag.

"Okay!" he said, "(_____)." I'll buy your stupid vegetables. But I only have one dollar."

She handed him a zucchini, but as she attempted to wrangle the tomato from the bottom of her bag, it fell to the ground. The train whipped past them, and he saw down her shirt a glance of her (_____). They called to him, like little fragrant berries from a mythical tree. He felt an unreasonable urge to put it in his (_____).

The (_____) was what got him. She'd gotten them a hotel room, one with dirty bedsheets and a picture of (_____) hanging lopsided on the wall. (_____) Stared at them as they fucked, his mouth dripping with (_____).

(Male 2) realized that (Woman) was lonely and volatile and was always trying to sell her vegetables to random men on the street. She was often turned down. Over the span of (_____), (Male 2) learned that (Woman) was very unaware of her proclivities toward (_____). She didn't know how badly she hurt herself. It was her sadness that compelled him to love her, which (Male 2) now realized was a (_____) to make up for his own (_____). It was like playing a game against himself that he would never win.

(Woman) continued to weep as he walked out of the hotel.

"(_____)," She said, grabbing at his ankles as he tried to walk out, sobbing. "(___ ___ ___)."

"I said no," (Male 2) said. He could still hear her crying as he walked down to the lobby, her wails rising above the polite piano music. He (_____) the way any person would (_____) after losing their (_____): like a lonely sock or a very misunderstood plunger.

(Male 2) worked at a flower shop. He had been working there for (_____), a family business passed down to him by his father. Women came to buy bouquets for (_____) or men to apologize for their wrongdoings. Some people would come by, alone, and buy a single flower. What did they do in their free time, and why did the single flowers make him so sad? He thought it to be (_____) in a way, though he knew that one shouldn't poeticize such a thing.

The worst thing was that he had massive, aching (_____). They hurt so bad that sometimes he wouldn't be able to concentrate, and would say things usually deemed socially unacceptable. He had done this once to the (_____) of the town, saying, "(_____)?" She had petitioned to have the flower shop shut down, but had given up due to the lack of support. People liked him. The flowers liked him, their (_____) opening as he walked into the store. And, of course, (Woman) liked him. He tried to remain in love with her, but (_____) made it hard. He never felt like singing any more, and they saw each other less. Now, threatened with the idea of their eruption, he felt as if he might as well just leave all of it — the shop, (Woman), the city, his car and his cat. But he didn't know where he would go. There were very few places to go where he wouldn't feel (_____), or that didn't remind him of (Woman o), who had set off on a trip to meet God one day and had never returned.

(Woman) wasn't crazy, just confused. She was confused about why she had a dog when she disliked dogs, confused about why she often bought clothes she had no attraction to, confused about why she always felt confused about her husband, (Male 1), who was by all means a very nice and attractive man. She wanted to believe that (_____) would come and transform her into a better person. A person who liked light (____), and little (____), and children who wore delight on their faces and dropped slimy bits of candy from their mouths onto the ground. But she never liked any of these things. She only liked (Male 2).

Being so full of emotion and regret for all the people she could not be, she often spent her days in the (_____). It cost $200 for a massage there, so she never paid for one. But she liked the feeling of being surrounded by (_____) and many naked women who did not know her but were perhaps just as unsure and full of fear as she. They would use nice grapefruit-scented scrubs on their (_____) legs, or chat about their outings. (Woman) didn't have any friends, but when she listened to these women, their various outings, looked at their (____) breasts, she would feel as if she were perhaps a part of these stories. She felt that maybe her (_____) were not the thing she had to offer, but instead offered things like kindness and comfort and humor to people who liked her.

The hot water made her feel better, as did the fact that everything was smeared with a thick white steam. It was as if she were in a film, and the (_____) was a (_____) through which she could travel and find her place in the world, maybe alongside of a woman with hair growing past her (_____) or a very large woman with (_____) (_____). On the nights she did not spend with (Male 2), she would fall asleep in the rooms upstairs, and dream of (_____): a very delicious sweet, one that many people adored and which she wished she could personify. And sometimes she dreamed of (Male 1), of course, but only out of (_____). When she would return from the bathhouse, he would preen himself like a (_____). He is always so happy to see her. In bed next to him, she feels like one of her (____): rotted, inedible, something once identifiable but now completely beyond use.

(Male 2) returns home to his apartment. His dog has been dead for approximately (____) days now. He has no room-mates. His (____) hurts. He remembers that (Male 1) knows of their affair and feels bile rising in his chest. He goes to vomit, his (_____) dragging along the wooden floors.

As he vomits up (_____), he attempts to tell himself a story. In the story, (Woman) and him have opened up a hybrid vegetable and flower shop. They live happily in a town by (_____), and her nipples are always shining and glorious. She will have no need to be sad or scared any more. (Male 1) will have moved on with little harm done to his ego or psyche. (Male 1) and he might even be friends. They will have (_____) together on summer nights, and he will give his blessing to their relationship.

His fantasy does not work. The vomit comes out of his (_____). He remembers himself a weak man, a plain man, a man not worth touching or knowing and solely known for the beautiful flowers he sells, which he does not resemble in any way.

After he has cleaned himself off and climbs into his (_____), he feels a sinking in his chest. There is a doubtless (_____) awaiting him, and one that will not stop until he is killed.

(Woman) feels it is perhaps more loving than it is heartless to just never return home. She does not want to imagine the look on (Male 1's) face, its vast and porous sorrow. She drives around in the parking lot of a grocery store for hours and hours. The cashiers leave from their shifts and glance at her, this (_____) woman doing donuts in the parking lot. She thinks about ramming her car into the building. She thinks of this pain as being more painful than a (_____).

She should not have made fun of (Male 1) for his balding hairline. She should not have fallen in love with a man to whom she sold a vegetable, although this was her usual tactic. It could have been anyone, someone who would have rejected her love and told her to return to her loving husband. But instead, she fell in love with (Male 2), although right now, she does not remember why. She can't remember why no matter how many times she circles

(_____)

around the parking lot. She wails, the sound a (_____)
blaring through the night.

(Male 2) begins preparing for his final moments. His phone
has not rung at all today, and he wants to know if perhaps
(Woman) is panicking as much as he is. Is she dead? Is she
taking a (____)? Has she made up with (Male 1), are they
fucking, what right does he have to ask such questions
when he is the one who has done what he has? He sells
(_____), (_____), (_____) to women and men with gleeful
smiles on their faces. It is close to (_____), a holiday which
he dreads, as he can never celebrate with her the way he'd
like.

As he closes up shop, not yet receiving a single text
from her, he decides to not be a (_____), not this time. For
once in his life, he will do the right thing. He gets into his
car. In one mile, past the tombstone and its daisies and the
loved ones buried and scattered across the grass, he will
arrive at their home. And he will say (or believes he will
say): "(_____)." And afterward, he will die.

(Woman) eventually returns home at 3 am. She realizes she
cannot avoid this moment, this vast (_____) inside of her.
Believes that she must, for once, face the fact of (_____).
As a child, her mother often told her of her multitude of
(_____), and though she'd like to blame all of her prob-
lems on this and other such tragedies, she thinks it is time to
no longer be a child. She thinks it is time to curry favor with
(_____).

As she pulls into the driveway, she sees (Male 2's) car there. She sits unmoving, dumbstruck, her body tense with fear that she may not be able to do this after all. A light is on inside of the living room, and two heads move in sync with one another. She closes her (__) and walks into the door backwards. In this way, she is performing strength. In this way, she will be able to allow them to see the most vulnerable part of her: her (___), its awful smoothness, the lie of softness on her skin.

<hr>

(Male 1) and (Male 2) watch as (Woman) walks into the house. She has placed her hands over her eyes, and she does not look at them as she continues moving backwards into the (_____).

(Male 2) shakes, the gun cold against his head. Why he chose to sacrifice himself in this way, he is not sure. She is actually a very terrible person. She actually only has her nipples and her sadness, and those do not account for much in this world.

(Male 1) sees this somehow. The fact that (Male 2) no longer loves his wife. This fills him with an (___) sadness and he begins to cry. A kind of domino effect ripples through the house, and soon, the walls are shaking with the wailing of three people in unison. He lowers the gun. He places it inside of his (_____).

<hr>

(Woman) realizes something, sitting there in the dark, waiting for the gun to fire. Though she did not see it, she is sure it will happen or something similar. She begins

(_____)

(_____), crying as she does. Something about all of this fills her with a sick pleasure. Gingerly, she picks up a (_____) from the pile of vegetables beside her, (_____) it down her throat. She dies from asphyxiation. In her final moments, she imagines herself as one of the women in the (_____): loved, surrounded by friends. She dies with a smile on her face, knowing this is not (_____).

(Male 1) and (Male 2) arrive in the bedroom, prepared for mourning. Both turn to the other, announcing the same things.

"I have respected what you did for my wife."

"May we all be (_____) in another world."

The woman they both loved, now dead, stares up into the ceiling. She is unable to see the way they join arms, walk backwards out of the flat with each covering the others' eyes. Had she been alive still, she would recognize this as a kind of (_____), a guardianship of another that she has never known. But instead, she remains blind to them. They smile all the way, leading themselves into the fortunate waves of the ocean. Together, they carefully make the fall. Their palms are sweaty. Their hands, for once, feel forgiven.

MACHINE TRANSLATION

For G.M.

The grand prize was $6,000 and we were broke. It wasn't a secret. I was embarrassed of everything she made, but especially of the thing she was entering for the contest. Mom called it the Frankenchine, which in reality, was this stupid-freezer shaped thing that could only appeal to people with time and money to spare, which I guess was everyone in this city except for us. Put in a shoe, a chair, whatever, and then leave it in the freezer for 15 minutes or so. When you took it out, it would have turned into something else entirely. When she wasn't home, my brother Mike and I had put in an old science textbook he had from middle school. It came back out as a cake. Every time we cut into it, we could hear the squeals of dolphins. The blue frosting tasted of ocean water and brine.

Mom used to have dreams and apprehensions, wanted to become something other than a mother. She never said it, but I knew that's how she felt. Over and over again, she'd show us pictures of her younger self, slim and fashionably dressed, laying around on the grass with her friends at Tokyo Institute of Technology. She'd gotten her PhD in Electronic Engineering, she'd say, proudly. Her dissertation was on Marxism and data infrastructure, risk transference; the need to reclaim technology from the bourgeoisie so that it could be used to disperse resources and information and even food. It had featured something like a precursor to the Frankenchine. And what did all of this get her? A job as a data analyst at a company that went against all of her beliefs about the evils of capitalism. It paid almost nothing. Each day, she looked even more defeated than the last. Life had stopped holding promise.

But Mom was determined in a way that sometimes frightened me. On the day of the competition, we showed up at 11 AM, only an hour before it was supposed to start. Mom had spent all night testing, retesting. Putting in our leftover dinner (canned meat came back in the form of a weird chimera thing—docile, though, so we kept it in the yard for a little before it ran away), her old reading glasses (portrait of some lady reading a collection of Yeats' poems wearing Mom's glasses). Then she went into her room and came back with Dad's old watch. We held our breaths as she placed it inside. But when she opened it, nothing came back out. "We'll just wait and see," she said. As I walked back from the bathroom at night, she was still there. Staring into the cold and empty cavern, hoping he might appear.

Mom, Mike, and I struggled to carry it up the stairs to the entrance. People walked past, their flashy inventions floating behind them, carried by huge drones. Something swooped overhead and the three of us ducked. I squinted up and saw a woman riding atop a golden bird the size of a small jet. It opened its chrome beak and spat confetti at us. The collar on its neck said "Frank." How could the Frankenchine would against him?

We paused for half a second as Frank glided into the colosseum, landing with ease at the registration table before turning into a small golf cart. There was a burst of applause. Confetti stuck to one of my eyelids. It smelled like peaches.

I was glad I couldn't see Mom's face as we started moving again. The Frankenchine couldn't fly. It could spit out confetti, though, but only if you fed it the right thing. "Fuck them," Mom mumbled under her breath. "We will win."

But the damp August heat made our hands slippery. Mike, younger than me but still much larger, was carrying the bulk of the weight from behind. *Just a couple more minutes. Just a couple more minutes, and then you can put it down,* I kept saying, but my fingers could no longer hold. Mike and I stared at each other, panicked, as the Frankenchine toppled over, taking Mike with it.

Mom screamed and rushed down the steps. Instead of running over to Mike, she watched in silence as the Frankenchine began sparking white fire. Two men rushed down with fire extinguishers, covering it with foam.

Mike was still on the stairs, breathing heavily, as I reached to pick him up.

"Are you okay?" I asked.

"Yeah." He winced. "I'm fine."

At the bottom of the stairs, Mom had sunk down to her knees. I hated to see her so embarrassed, so disappointed. She was always embarrassed—never enough money, aging rapidly despite all the skincare products she bought, kids who only ever excelled at being average, thinking of herself as stupid, stupid, stupid because no one ever told her how smart she was. Which was the same attitude with which she now viewed us.

All of it made me sad. The way her hatred of us was an extension of herself, the fact that she was aware of her cruelty but didn't know how to stop it. I placed a hand on her shoulder.

"Don't touch me, Marcus," she said. I could tell that she was crying. So I left her alone. I helped Mike, limping with his newly sprained ankle, toward the car. The Frankenchine was still smoking as we passed by it.

We waited by the car for a long time. Eventually, Mom showed up.

Wordlessly, she unlocked the door and we got into the backseat. She started the car, and we sat there, stalling in the parking lot. I heard a knock on the window.

"Do you want to keep these? I'm very sorry, ma'am." The man was holding up two plastic bags full of black metal, all that remained of her work.

"Yes," I started saying, but then Mom interrupted me.

"No," she said, and I tried not to look at her not looking at them from the rearview mirror. Her grey hair fell to cover her eyes. "But thank you. Thank you very much."

After that, Mom started calling out of work almost every week, or leaving early to come back home, immediately shutting herself into the office without saying anything to us. Eventually, her work spilled out into the living room, taking over the entire floor. Mike and I developed a conscious way of forgetting that the living room existed.

Once, after coming back from getting snacks at the corner store, he'd bumped into the couch. It startled both of us. "I didn't even remember it was there," he'd whispered as we walked down the narrow hallway toward our rooms, still hearing the electrical hums from Mom's office. "I really didn't."

Then one night, I'd pushed through the apartment door, angry at a fight I'd just had with my girlfriend at the time. She didn't understand, she said. You liked me before, so why can't you like me now? She was talking about the fact that I was gay. She refused to believe it, telling me it was perhaps just a phase, until I finally dipped, left her screaming after me on the park bench.

Something was different in the house. I paused, trying to figure out what it was. Mom was usually up until 5 AM or so, working, punching things in, taking it apart, putting it back together, until she passed out and then got up again at 7 to go to work. But now, it was completely silent.

I took a step toward the forbidden zone, pausing before I turned the handle. If she were inside, she would be furious. And then we'd never have the chance to talk about anything important. We never did. *I have to do it now*, I thought, and pushed the door open.

Mom wasn't there. But something else was: pulsing, humming, a steady rhythm of blue lights. It seemed like a mistake, that she'd leave something on. I went to turn it off, ignoring the fact that Mike and I would surely be jostled awake in the morning. *What did I tell you two about touching my stuff? Eh? Why can't you just listen?*

The screen was unlocked—also strange. Mom was suspicious of everything, everyone: grocery store clerks, bankers, neighbors. *Don't ever trust anyone*, she often said.

Ever. There must have been at least five layers of security verifications to go through.

Something is wrong, something is wrong. My heart rate spit out irregular rhythms. On the unlocked menu interface, six options glowed before me:

認知地図【自動】
関係データベース
上書き
逆符号化
Log

I didn't want to see this. Where was the off button? But no matter where I looked, there was simply nothing. There was no off option. I tried to walk away, wanted to. Instead, I pressed the first option.

The screen suddenly filled with complicated diagrams, equations, notes. I swiped through, barely looking, feeling something bloating inside of my stomach, threatening to burst.

Suddenly, I heard Mom snoring. She hadn't snored in years, ever since they had put her on Anxiolytics. I hoped whatever she was dreaming of was free of what she sought in waking life: all the different possibilities of betrayal.

A notebook lay open on a nearby table. I grabbed it, trying to make sense of the first page.

"Miscommunication...intuitive emotional understanding...chasm of inevitable corruption...forgotten modes of relation...imminent transactional nature of human interconnection..."

I kept swiping through. Initial diagrams showed a small cube, the processor. You input the following: Name, date, place of birth, gender, race, relationship with the following, how long you had known them.

I read faster, twenty pages of notes, feeling as if I were falling apart. The machine would then search all of the available data online about this person: Search history. Family background. Purchases. Social media usage. Medical and job history. Communication patterns pulled from texts and emails with other people.

The last page of the notes featured one last small addition.

Input transcripts of any conversations you have had, in person or otherwise.

So that's what she had been doing all this time. Figuring out a way to translate other people's emotions into something she could understand. Looking past all the niceties, the lies, the half-truths and platitudes, to get to the truth.

The snoring continued, but quieter. Who was this woman? I was terrified of the person sleeping in the twin-sized mattress right next door. How had this person who once cared so much about protecting others, wanting to see people more unified, less broken, become this?

Scrambling back to the machine, I swiped to an option that read "relationship database."

Jimmy Zhang
Chiyoko Hanada
Mamoru Matsumoto

Taiichi Tomiya
Anna Takemura
Yasuhiro Okada

The names were ones I recognized; friends from her program, graduate school, grandpa, her best friend from childhood. Most of them were dead now.

The last name was my father's name.

She had told us she was no longer in contact with him, that she no longer cared. Everyone knew it was a lie, and now here was the truth laid bare. Hundreds of past entries unraveled onscreen, starting all the way back from eight years ago. The texts. Emails. And then, their translations. Mom had documented notes in the corner, more and more frenzied as I swiped through. I didn't want to read the messages; what was I looking for? I toggled over to the log.

Yasuhiro claims that he has not found anyone new, prompting me to move forward with this experiment after having put it aside for many years. While everything is still in working order, further adjustments are needed to ensure veracity of results. I hope to help not only myself gain closer understanding of those around me, but also, should this be successful, present a newer model for public usage. 04/08/2012

It became obvious today that Yasuhiro might suspect that I am using our conversations for something, but he isn't sure what. Having already inserted this into the database, I am sure this will yield more answers. Suspicion seems to imply some kind of guilt or secrecy. 12/25/2012

Yasuhiro stated today that he misses the children. But in

the past three years, he has only mentioned them two times, and only when prompted (03/12/2003, 04/28/2004). Their names don't appear in his search history, and recent messages in the past week with colleagues and friends have solely been business related. Emotional patterns with above mentioned relations remain ultimately stable, no suggestion of isolation, withdrawal, volatility or excess. 2/22/2013.

As of two months ago, I have noticed a change in his emotional relation to one woman in particular. His purchase history indicates the two are romantically involved; I.e., movie tickets, beauty product purchases, lingerie. Although all of the indexing has been completed for their most recent conversations earlier today, I have not been able to look at them yet. I have begun to doubt the urgency of belief with which I first started out in this project. Now, I believe it can do only harm. 04/20/2013.

I swiped to the messages from today, between her and my father.

04/20/2013

Hello Read 1:30 pm
Hello, Yasuhiro. How are you today? Read 3:30 pm
Please forgive my asking. I miss you every day.
Do you miss me? Or have you found someone else? 3:45

Mirai-chan, I'm sorry for not responding earlier. I was busy with work. But the answer is yes, of course. Of course I miss you, every day.

I think about you all the time, even though things became what they were. I'm sorry. I'm sorry to not know what Mike and Marcus are up to now. I promise I'll visit one day soon. Eventually, maybe, we can be a family again. I love you always...always, always. Will respond more later. 11:46 PM

TRANSLATION:
MIRAI I AM SORRY I AM IN LOVE WITH ANOTHER WOMAN I DON'T MEAN TO HURT YOU I FEEL GUILT I FEEL SADNESS I FEEL SHAME I FEEL A SENSE OF UNRAVELING AT ALL WE COULD NOT HOLD I DO NOT KNOW IF I EVER LOVED YOU BUT I THINK I LOVED WHAT WE HAD IN THE TIME WE DID DO NOT FEEL AS IF THIS WERE YOUR FAULT I AM NEVER COMING TO VISIT I WILL FORGET MARCUS I WILL FORGET MIKE IN TIME I WILL FORGET YOU

I thought about my mother standing here earlier today, reading these words. I thought about my mother not looking at the men when they had asked if she wanted to take the pieces of the Frankenchine home, her blank disposition in the face of pain.

It was already 7 AM, and the sun was splitting my head open. *Tomorrow*, I thought, *I'll be a good son, I'll go check on her.*

I woke up at 2 PM. Rain paused on the window before quivering down.

Mike stood in my doorway, wearing my old soccer jersey. He had something to say, I could tell. I didn't want to know. I turned away, facing the rain again, thinking about the different wires splintering inside my mind, the invisible wires that connected us to each other becoming frayed, split, cut open. I focused on each individual raindrop, watching them travel downwards, ignoring Mike as, over and over again, he wailed in his stupid fucking kid voice, "Mom's dead. Mom's dead. Mom's dead."

We lived at our aunt's house for a while. I don't remember much of those hazy beginning days. At her funeral, there were only five of us: My aunt, Mike, and myself, as well as two people she seemed to have known from work. One of the women wore bright blue eyeshadow that ran down her face as she spoke. "I always knew something like this would happen," the woman with blue eyeshadow said to us before the other woman shushed her, pointing at us and shaking her head.

So it was true. I hated the way that the women spoke of her, after the service was over: this woman who could have been brilliant had it not been for her brain. Which parts of it were brilliant, and which parts of it were diseased? I wanted to scream at them. What's the difference?

As we grew older, Mike and I became enmeshed in our own worlds of obsession. Mike went on to study French history at Yale, always too busy with his research to give me a phone call. I took up pottery class at a local community center, led by a beautiful guy named Jack. He had the most delicious brown curls I'd ever seen. I loved the way the clay felt as I spun it into different shapes; thin-necked birds, flattened embossed plates, swooping pitchers that I would then place inside a hot oven until complete. At one of the first classes I took, I suddenly had a wild feeling that after we took them out, they'd be transformed entirely, into different beings. But the oven was just an oven, and Mom was gone.

Everything I made was terrible at the beginning, but after a year, I made something that showed promise: a sculpture that I titled "Fortune's Favorite:" a pair of sorrowful-looking women dancing, their heads twisted away from one another as they gazed, in terror or awe, into separate parts of the sky. Their robes disappeared into a sprawl of gardenias, wild animals, and broken pieces of glass.

"Marcus, you should enter this into the Arizona Art competition." I was standing with Jack in his studio. He was kind but never dishonest; he didn't believe in false praise. When we'd first gotten drinks, and went back to his place afterward, I'd started shaking as we got into bed. He thought he'd done something wrong. *No,* I'd said. *I'm just embarrassed. Embarrassed of what?* He'd asked, stroking my hair. *I don't deserve it.* I'd said. He cupped my face in his hands, forcing my face up. And then he'd smiled. *What a stupid thing to say.* And then, *Hating yourself is one thing. But don't expect me to hate you too.*

"It's not that great," I said. "I'll just give it away to someone, or sell it."

"Can you stop saying that?"

"I don't know what you mean. I don't think there's anything wrong with just wanting to make people happy."

He turned away from me and grabbed a paper towel, wiping his hands. "If you don't do it, I'm going to enter for you."

"You won't do that."

"I will, Marcus, and you know it."

"God. Can you just stop?"

He threw the paper towel in the trash, his jaw hardened. "I know your shit is good. Every time I say something good about you, you immediately tell me I'm wrong."

"I can see how that's hurtful."

"Marcus," he said, and now his eyes were soft, like crumbling red clay. "Stop underestimating yourself."

I started walking toward the car. From behind, I heard him call out, "I've already entered you by the way, so we should hear back by next month. And if we don't get this one, you'll get the next."

I wasn't optimistic. I knew there were people more talented than me, less depressed, more passionate about devoting time to their art, rather than sleeping and waking up to go to work at the organic grocery store and doing it all over again.

I woke up at 6 AM. Tomorrow was supposed to be the day I heard back. I'd spent the night looking up ways to fall asleep; all of which suggested things that I'd already tried: melatonin, exercise, more of certain greens or nuts. I kept bringing home supplements from work, to the point where there was no more room left in Jack's medicine cabinet. As I pawed through the different bottles, I found one I didn't remember getting, a dark green bottle for sleep, as well as memory and brain performance. *Take one capsule 30 minutes before bedtime on an empty stomach.* I shook it, but it was empty.

At first, I'd been angry at him for entering me, but then

I'd realized: *No one else has ever advocated for you before. No one.* And then I'd stopped being mad.

Jack was already in the kitchen, making coffee.

"Today's the day you find out, right?" he said, sliding a cup out to me as I sat down.

"Yeah."

"I think you have a good chance. And don't say I'm jinxing you. I don't want to hear it."

We drank our coffee and I biked to work. On my lunch break, I saw an email in my inbox.

Sender: ARIZONA COALITION FOR THE ARTS
Subject: Regarding your 2025 Arizona Arts Coalition Contest submission

For a second, I thought about deleting it, pretending I'd never seen it. I'd tell Jack that I hadn't gotten in and that we could try again next year. But then I saw the first line: "Congratulations." I couldn't stop shaking. *Mike will be so happy,* and then I had a vision: Mom standing on the bleachers, cheering at the top of her lungs, calling out our names, even when we'd already lost.

My mind sinking, I looked at the email again to figure out the details, but there were none. "Congratulations," it said, and that was all.

That weekend, Jack and I drove from Phoenix to Tucson. *See? All the info is right there,* he'd said, showing me the website. There would be an exhibition for myself and the two others who had won: a man in his early 50's who'd built the city of Shanghai out of fibers, and an installation artist who'd created an army of Russian fairytale figures from discarded plastic and lightbulbs. *Their intern probably fucked up.* But they hadn't responded, even after I'd sent another email confirming my attendance. Still, Jack kept saying we should go. There were plenty of great artists over the years who had won.

"I'd never even heard of it before you mentioned it to me," I said, but as I spoke, the names and faces of previous winners came back to me instantly.

"We'll be fine," Jack said, yawning. "Worst case, it's a scam, and you'll still get to put 'Third-place winner of the AACC' on your CV. Hell, maybe we should just start making up organizations. I bet so many people already do."

Still, I felt more scared than I did excited. The nausea hadn't gone away. Jack slept next to me in the car, his head resting against the windowpane as trees raced us to the finish line.

When we'd looked at the website, the directions had pointed us to the Tucson Art and Science Museum. But when I'd put the address in my phone, all that showed up was a dilapidated looking building. We were already halfway there.

I stopped at a gas station.

"Do you want me to get you anything?" I asked Jack, but he was still asleep. His brows were furrowed as he twisted away from my touch, mumbling.

Inside, I put two waters on the counter and asked for a pack of Marlboro Reds. As the woman turned to get them, suddenly I felt a sharp pulsing in the back of my head, as if my brain were trying to remember something.

"You okay?" The middle-aged white woman asked, frowning.

"Yeah," I said. "Do you know anything about the Tucson Art and Science Museum?"

She shrugged, handing me the plastic bag. "I don't really know much about that stuff, to be honest. Last time I went to a museum was when I took my grandkids to the Air and Space Museum."

"Thanks." I gave her exact change and she went back to looking at her phone.

There was a house directly across the street, its slats were painted a sickly green. A small wooden fence jutted haphazardly out of the ground like rows of rotting teeth. I lit a cigarette and smoked it as fast as I could before stomping it out on the wet curb.

"Hey," I said, "I feel really weird. Maybe we should just head back home." But Jack was still tossing in his sleep, unresponsive. I backed out of the parking lot, taking one last look at the house before driving away.

We passed more houses, gas stations, sad little strip malls. There was only 20 minutes to go, but I still felt freaked out. At the stoplight, a man looked over at me from his car. Perhaps it was the shape of his face, like a rounded globe, or maybe just the expression it held: as if the soul had been discarded long ago. Either way, I froze, unable to hear the sounds of the cars honking behind me.

I remembered this house somehow. I could see Mike and I getting into the backseat as Mom pulled out of the driveway. And then she had started driving fast, too fast. The radio was turned to the wrong channel, and static played from our speakers, turned to the highest volume. Mike had been terrified. "What's going on?" He'd cried as

Mom tapped out the rhythm to the static, her eyes vacant even as they scanned the road.

"Nothing is wrong," I'd said. "Just go to sleep." Mom kept driving fast and the static grew louder and louder until finally, our speakers shot out.

This was the first time I'd been able to recall Mom's face so vividly: her gritted teeth, the small crow's feet around her eyes, strands of hair stuck to her forehead with sweat. Unable to see her sons sitting scared in the car with her, unable to see anything but whatever played out before her on the highway.

But why had we been there? Had someone we'd known lived in that house? I kept driving, feeling my eyes bulge as I followed the directions without thinking. *Turn right. Make a U-turn. Go straight for 3.4 miles. Turn right. Continue straight. The destination will be on your left. You have arrived.*

I parked the car. There was nothing there except the skeleton of an old elementary school. Leaves and vines grew wild around the swings and tire toys. I shut the engine off, placing a foot onto the cracked asphalt. Where were we?

"Jack. I'm scared." I shook him. His snores grew even louder. "Jack, wake up."

But he didn't. Everything was okay, though. It had to be. "Alright. Well, we probably just made a wrong turn somewhere. I'm sorry."

I turned the car on and started backing up. But it wasn't moving. Hyperventilating, I sunk down into the seat just as I saw a figure slinking toward us in the rearview mirror. It was a boy, slowly making his way toward the playground. A bad bowl cut, dark brows, wearing a jersey with the name of a soccer team on it. My middle school soccer team. I screamed.

"No, please," I begged him, "Please don't turn around." But he'd dropped something, and I saw what was written on the back, just enough to make out the tops of the letters: MATSUMOTO.

"Marcus." His voice was high and clear as he came to the window, a concerned look on his face as he peered through the glass. "Are you alright?"

"What—who are you?"

"We don't have time for this," he said, cutting me off, and I saw his lip curl in the same way mine did whenever I was trying not to cry. "Do you want to see what Mom was doing?"

"What happened to Jack? What did she do to Jack?"

"She didn't do anything to him," he said sadly. "It was me. I made the website. I made Jack think it was real. But he's not dead, don't worry. It's just until we're gone."

"'We'? Please. Please. I don't know what you mean. Mom died six years ago. I don't know how you exist, how she made you, but you're not me. I'm me." I stopped to catch my breath. "I'm me."

My voice echoed around us, into the emptiness of the school grounds. Tears now streamed down the boy's face as he came closer. I flinched and he backed away, crying even harder.

"I know I'm not you, Marcus," he said. "But I'm Marcus. I know I am. I have all of your memories. Go ahead, ask me one."

"How much worse has it gotten?" I asked, not knowing what I was saying. "What's gotten worse?"

The kid didn't respond, but I couldn't pretend any more. Guilt poured from his face, and I knew he was me.

I'd seen myself with this exact expression in the photographs someone had taken at Mom's funeral.

Suddenly, he jumped at an invisible noise.

"Mike?" he called out, his voice full of fear. "Mike, what's happening?" He began running toward the ruins.

"Mike's here?" I thought about my brother, his studies, the way we'd lost touch over the years. My heart broke. I wanted to see him. *I don't have anything to do with this,* I thought to myself. *Leave them to deal with all this shit, like me and Mike had to.* But all our lives, there'd been nothing but cowards; people who'd failed us. Failed our mother.

"I'll be right back," I said to Jack. His long lashes fluttered, as if trying to open. "I'm going to lock the door. I love you." Then I ran toward the school, not bothering to look behind me.

The walls smelled like mildew. Water leaked from holes in the ceiling, but I recognized the walls. This was the where my locker was, this was the room I'd had history class in. But both me and Mike had gone to the same high school in Phoenix for the entire four years. I traced back in my mind to those years. Me passing by Mike in the hallway, slapping him upside the head. Mike waiting for me outside by the bike racks so that we could go back home. But what did we see as we biked home? What were the things we passed by? There was nothing but a curtain of white, stretched out in every direction around us. Something shuddered in my memory, and our apartment appeared, the same one we'd lived in forever. But it seemed blurred now that I was in this place, a kind of schism filtering out something else. I pushed my mind to go past it. The apartment fell, revealing the eerie house we'd passed by on our way here. And now I remembered where I knew it from.

How could I have forgotten that we had moved, briefly, to Tucson? She had gotten a job. No, that wasn't it. She had come here for a job, and it hadn't worked out. She'd started working as an administrative assistant at a community college. Marcus and I spent so many days inside, not wanting to go out, afraid of our new surroundings. And Mom had known. She'd come back home one day, and all I could think of now was her voice, "Here, Mike. Something to help you feel better." A white substance falling in droplets onto my tongue...

"Marcus?" It was a surreal feeling, to be calling out to myself. "Marcus, where are you?"

I heard noises, a child's shrieking, from the end of the hallway. This was the science room, it had to be it. Mike and I had both cut open frogs there. I found another forgotten memory: Mike's face as he told me how gross it was, sticking out his tongue, his nose scrunched up in fake disgust. It seemed so sad, to have lost that moment.

The smell of formaldehyde grew stronger as I approached the door. I walked inside.

"Mom, please stop. He's going to die," Marcus pled. He'd spread his body over the unmoving form on the metal table, as if trying to protect it from the pretty woman who now lurched toward him, zombie-like. A glass vial shattered and hit the wall behind them. I hadn't realized I was even holding it. Mom spun around to look at the intruder, frantic and confused.

She was so young. A version of Mom I'd never known, who'd existed before she'd had us, regarded me with glazed eyes. How did I feel? I missed her. I hated her. I wanted her to not leave us behind. But these familiar emotions shifted to terror as I saw her drift back toward the table, where Marcus had crumpled to the floor, trembling. Neatly, calmly, her hands carved a sharp incision into Mike's already flayed stomach. Before I knew it, I had tackled her. Blood, not mine, but someone else's, dripped down my arm as I pinned her to the floor.

"Where is it?" she murmured to herself. Could she really not recognize me? *It isn't really Mom*, I thought. But it hurt all the same.

"Honey, you have to relax," she called out to Marcus. "All I want to do is understand you more. That's all I want."

"You never wanted to understand," I screamed. It didn't matter if she wasn't Mom, she was Marcus and Mike's mom, and was still the fucking same. I grabbed a pair of scissors, holding them over her face, but her eyes remained distant, dreaming. "You never wanted to fucking understand us."

"Mike," I heard my younger self whimper. "Mike is dying."

"Marcus, honey," Mom sang. "Won't it be great when I can understand you two? Then I can always be sure to be kind. Then I can be sure to always make you happy, to never misunderstand you. I'll never die, we'll live forever..."

I watched her fingers lift into the air, expecting them to reach out toward Marcus, but instead, she reached up to my head, smoothing my hair. I broke. Holding the scissors in my hands, I plunged them downward into her chest.

There was a brief moment in time where Mom had started trying to see someone else. He was a large Japanese guy who brought us Ferrero Rocher chocolates each time he came over. We didn't hate him. The more he stuck around, the more we started thinking of him as a replacement father, who by that point, we had already started forgetting, anyway.

Six months into their relationship, he suddenly stopped coming around.

"We're going on a walk," Mom said. She was wearing a large sunhat that eclipsed her entire face. "Put on your shoes."

"Is Ryonosuke-san coming over?" Mike asked. Usually, we only went on walks when he came over.

"No," Mom said. "He can't make it today."

We walked around our neighborhood, looping around and around the block. Mom was skinny and out of shape, she had to keep asking Mike and I to stop running off. So we tried to walk slower. It was weird to be having this thing with her, this "outing." We never went on vacations. We ate most of our meals in silence. Mike kept glancing at her nervously, trying to figure out what was wrong.

"Is everything okay?" I asked as Mom got the keys out of her pocket, unlocking the door.

"What do you mean?"

"I mean, is everything okay with Ryonosuke-san?"

She sighed, taking off the sunhat and placing it on the cluttered mail table. It had left a crease in the middle of her forehead. "He told me that he was in love with me. That he wanted to be my world." She snorted. "Who asked for anything like that? So creepy. I told him, 'My sons are my world. My sons are the only world I need.'"

"Marcus," Mom whispered. She was slumped against the chalkboard, each breath labored. *This isn't really her,* I kept reminding myself, but she was looking straight at me, her eyes alert for the first time.

"I don't get it," I said. My mind was fracturing; I couldn't pull myself out of my thoughts. "I don't understand. Why do I have to watch you die for the second time? I don't understand."

"Marcus," she said again, looking at me in such innocent awe. The open sky above us had begun to darken, and shadows curved around her face. "My baby boy. How did you get so old?" She struggled to stand up, but the wound was too deep. She was dying. "Did I do something wrong?" she pleaded. "Are you and Mikey hurt?"

I wanted to tell her yes. I wanted to tell her about all the hurt she'd caused us, that the pain lasts forever. I wanted to tell her it was better off that she wasn't ever alive.

And I would have meant all of it.

I moved toward where the chalkboard stood, on the other side of the wall, but she kept reaching for me, begging: "What's wrong? What happened? What's wrong? Are you and Mikey hurt?"

Watching her, this younger version of Mom who I'd never known, a shock thrilled through my spine. She'd known all along how terrible a mother she was. She hated herself for it; didn't know what to do about it. So she never said a thing. At some point, during our life in Tucson, she must have created these versions of ourselves to learn from them. Learn how she might become a better mother through studying this severed self.

This wasn't someone I could hate. She didn't deserve it. I started sobbing. I walked back over to her, carefully cradling her in my lap. Her eyes were fluttering, so I drew close. I wanted to make sure she could hear me.

"You did a great job. You've always been the best mom in the world."

"Really?" she asked, her words slurring together. Her eyes drifted shut. "I love you so much, son."

"I love you, too, Mom, I love you so much," I sobbed. "I love you so much. Mom, do you know that? Do you hear me?"

But her body was still. The words had come too late after all.

A movement in the corner of my eye. Marcus was crying. This was his mother, too, after all. I waved him over. The two of us sat there for a while, the cool night air drawing itself around us, not knowing what to do.

Perhaps in some ways, Mom had been right. Perhaps love was a thing outside of human time or imagination, and could reach further than we ever could to touch the dead.

Marcus was a lot smarter than I'd been as a kid. He'd spent the past year gathering data from different artists in the state, figuring out where I was. Eventually, he'd found Jack's studio and seen my name. Then he'd set to work in designing all of this: creating renders of sculptures and paintings, the fake coalition. He'd sent the email out to one person only: Jack. He'd found the scheduling system for my job and sent the bottle of supplements to Jack's place while I was gone. It had released into his system much later, as we were already on our way.

"It only lasts two days. I tested it out."

"On who?"

He looked away. "There were a lot of different Mikes over the years. So many I've lost count. But I think there's only been one of me. On five different Mikes, under relatively calm conditions, it yielded the same result.

"Don't worry," he said, seeing the expression on my face. "Even if we're a little different than you, we're still completely human."

"I'm sorry about Mike," I said. It felt funny to say out loud, in a sick way. I was sorry about his Mike, and, selfishly, mine too: how far away he felt now, probably so different than any past iterations of him I'd grown up with.

"It's okay." His smile was a sad smile, too aware, too tired for such a young kid to have. "I've gotten used to it."

"How did you learn how to do all of this?" We were getting closer now to where we'd spent the rest of the entire evening shoveling dirt for two burial plots, one for Mom, and one for Mike.

He looked at me as if I were stupid. "Mom taught me."

Both of us were too tired to cry. Marcus had dressed Mike in one of the shirts they kept in that row of lockers so that the gashes didn't show. We'd found a new lab coat for Mom. Both of them looked so gaunt. I couldn't get over the calm look on Mom's face. I'd never seen it before.

"I wonder if we should say something," Marcus said to me.

I opened my mouth, but no words came out. I shook my head. "I don't think there's anything to say."

He nodded and we packed them into the earth, until their faces were no longer visible, disappearing under the dirt. By the time we were finished, the sun had set, revealing a new day.

"She always talked about you, you know."

We were sitting in the car, waiting for Jack to wake up. Marcus had told me that he needed to be the one to handle the explanations, and I'd said that that was fine. The kid's mind was incredible; so fast even with no sleep.

Jack snored softly as Marcus continued. "She told me she hadn't done it right the first time. Loving the other versions of us. And there had been another version of her, too, but she'd died. But not before making sure there was a backup plan, and now she was going to make everything alright.

"I think your mom even came to visit us one day."

I jolted. "What was she like?"

"I don't remember very well. But it's one of the first memories I can recall. She kept looking at us and crying. I asked if something were wrong, but she just kept saying that it would be different this time. That she'd take better care of us. I didn't understand anything she was saying. I started thinking I'd imagined it, that maybe they were just the same person. But that woman had looked older. And then I read the obituary online, about your mom. How she died..." His voice trailed off. It was still fresh for him, Mom's death. I imagined that tomorrow was when all the emotions would finally sink in.

"I'm so sorry," I said. A stupid platitude, one that I'd heard so many times throughout my life.

He shook his head. "Me too."

A breeze was picking up now, leaves sticking to the windows. Apparently, people in the area said that the elementary school was haunted. No one ever came except for teenagers, and Marcus had created a whole show for them.

"It was some really scary shit," he said, grinning. I

recognized that expression, of course, that devious one. It had just been so long since I'd worn it myself. "You'll just have to trust me."

"I'm sure."

His face turned serious. "Mom was the most brilliant person in the world," Marcus said.

"Yes."

"You don't have to take me with you, you know."

"Yes," I said. "I do."

There was a groan. Jack stretched, wincing as he rubbed his shoulders.

"Jesus Christ. How long was I asleep for?" He looked outside of the window. "Did we get lost?"

"Hello, Jack," Marcus said, ducking in between us from the backseat.

Jack screamed, jumping in his chair. "What the fuck? Oh my God. What the fuck? Marcus, who the hell is this kid?"

"Hey. It's okay," Marcus said, unfazed by his reaction. He'd been through so much more than I had. It made me feel guilty: compared to him, I'd lived through nothing. "I know it's confusing, but I have to be the one to explain everything."

"Huh?" Jack's eyes darted over to me. "Marcus. Come on, what—"

"Remember that supplement you took a while ago, at your place?" Marcus asked. Jack nodded. "Good. It's going make it easier for you to absorb what I'm going to say. He can't tell you, because I'm the smarter one."

Marcus winked at me, and then began.

NOTES

THE RABBIT GOD

1. **Fragment**
   You stand on the bridge overlooking the landscape,
   and upstairs someone looking at the landscape looks at you.
   The moon adorns your window,
   and you adorn somebody's dream.
   — "Fragment", Bian Zhillin, trans. Lucas Klein: *Cha Journal*.
   February 16, 2021.
2. "Excerpt from *The Peddler*", He Qifang, trans. Canaan Morse: *Paper Republic: Chinese Literature in Translation*. July 15, 2008.

ACKNOWLEDGMENTS

There are too many people in this world I have to thank for keeping me alive, for keeping me writing. Even at my most difficult, you were there for me. You know who you are, whether or not you are still in my life; whether or not you are still on this earth.

Although I am sure to forget some, here are a few:

Jana, Mona, Christopher, Vi, Jess, Ali, Mara, Jesi, Jacqui, Sasha, Lou, Ellen, Jake, Mar, Ivan, Crow, Ashleigh, Bud, Michael, Juliet, Elle, Scott, Joey, Karter, Sam, Ginger, Carlos, Celeste, Jamila, Fullamusu, Joseph, Howard, Steve, William, Hari, Muriel, Maggie, B.R., Cavin, Kant, Haolun, Jiaqi, Lis, Anthony, Ellen, Ivan, Matt, Talbott, Stanley, Mar, Ben, Jake, Max, Dileny, Richard, Princess, Ren T., Ren S., Lark, Conner, Armando, Daniel, Kev, Joe, Tevin, Christian F., Jonah, Bims, Patrick, René, Andrew, Brian, Fan, Funké, Leia, Nhu, Devan, Nic, Aidan, Danny, Amy, Simone, Mia, Wei, Leia, Caroline, Clare, Crane, Owen, Libby, K., Nathan, Micah, Jay, Thom, Connie, Peter, Reina, Thomas, Dustin, Caitlin, Jacob, Kathleen, David, Nami, Jill, Ross, Karen, Atsuko K., Atsuko N., Tamaki, Ryuta, Ichisei, Sachi, Andrew, Radhika, Eli, Linda, Janine, Carol, Julia, Peng, Olivia, Wendy

All of my friends and students and clients and editors, mentors and guides

Maudlin House, Autostraddle, Joyland Magazine, Brink Literary, Southwest Review, Tiding House, Sine Theta Magazine, and 128 *Lit* for publishing previous versions of some of these stories, as well as *X-R-A-Y Literary Magazine*

& you, for reading this

ABOUT THE AUTHOR

Daisuke Shen is the author of *Vague Predictions &
Prophecies* (CLASH Books 2024) and *Funeral,* co-authored
with Vi Khi Nao (KERNPUNKT Press 2023). They can
be found at www.daisukeshen.com

ALSO BY CLASH BOOKS

EARTH ANGEL

Madeline Cash

SILVERFISH

Rone Shavers

WITCH HUNT & BLACK CLOUD: NEW & COLLECTED WORKS

Juliet Escoria

INVAGINIES

Joe Koch

MARGINALIA

Juno Morrow

I'M FROM NOWHERE

Lindsay Lerman

SEPARATION ANXIETY

Janice Lee

HEXIS

Charlene Elsby

FLOWERS FROM THE VOID

Gianni Washington

WE PUT THE LIT IN LITERARY

CLASHBOOKS.COM

FOLLOW US

TWITTER

IG

FB

@clashbooks

Printed in the USA
CPSIA information can be obtained
at www.ICGtesting.com
JSHW021105290824
69014JS00004B/81